Dear Reader,

I'm very excited to be writing the launch title for Harlequin Flipside. Harlequin has taken the best of the genre known as "chick lit" and combined it with the enduring appeal of romance. The result is stories with a little edge and attitude, but with the happily-ever-after ending that most readers, including myself, insist on and love.

I hope you enjoy reading Francie and Mark's story, *Staying Single*. And I hope you liked meeting the wonderful and wacky Morelli family, whom you'll be seeing more of in Lisa Morelli's story coming in 2004. Lisa definitely marches to the beat of her own drum, and I hope you'll follow along behind her as she tries to unravel the mess her life has become.

As always, I would love to hear your comments on *Staying Single*, so please write to me at P.O. Box 41206, Fredericksburg, Virginia 22404 or visit my Web site at www.milliecriswell.com.

Best always,

Millie Criswell

"It looks big enough for two. It even might be queen-size."

Mark's gaze switched between the sofa bed and Francie, as if trying to gauge her reaction.

Optimism was all well and good, but she didn't think this was the time for it. It was one thing to be stranded in a *small* apartment overnight, but another thing entirely to have to share an even smaller bed.

"As much as I'd like to accommodate you, Mark, I don't think it would be a good idea to share this bed." How would she ever keep her hands off him?

"Tell you what. I promise to be on my best behavior. You can go in the bathroom and change. I'll close my eyes until you're safely under the covers, then I'll hop in. How does that sound?"

It sounded indecently delicious, but she wasn't about to tell him that.

"I don't know...."

"Please? I'm too old and too much of a wuss to sleep on the floor." He reinforced his plea with a persuading grin that she was incapable of resisting.

She was *so* in trouble....

Millie Criswell

Staying Single

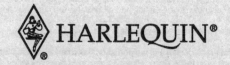

HARLEQUIN®

TORONTO • NEW YORK • LONDON
AMSTERDAM • PARIS • SYDNEY • HAMBURG
STOCKHOLM • ATHENS • TOKYO • MILAN • MADRID
PRAGUE • WARSAW • BUDAPEST • AUCKLAND

To Stef Ann Holm:

Thank you for your friendship and support.
And for being my dieting buddy!

ISBN 0-373-44175-4

STAYING SINGLE

Visit us at www.eHarlequin.com

Printed in U.S.A.

ABOUT THE AUTHOR

Millie Criswell, *USA TODAY* bestselling author and winner of a *Romantic Times* Career Achievement Award and a National Readers Choice Award, has published over twenty-three romance novels. She began her writing career when her husband uttered those prophetic words: "Why don't you try writing one of those romances you're always reading?" Knowing that her dream of tap dancing with the Rockettes wasn't likely to materialize—due to a lack of dancing talent—Millie jumped on the idea with both feet, so to speak, and has been charming readers with hilarious stories and sparkling characters ever since. Millie resides in Virginia with her husband and loveable Boston terrier.

Books by Millie Criswell

Don't miss any of our special offers. Write to us at the following address for information on our newest releases.

Harlequin Reader Service
U.S.: 3010 Walden Ave., P.O. Box 1325, Buffalo, NY 14269
Canadian: P.O. Box 609, Fort Erie, Ont. L2A 5X3

Dear Reader,

Welcome to Harlequin Flipside! If you love a dash of wit and cleverness with your romance, then this is the line for you. These stories are for readers who appreciate that, if love makes the world go around, the ride is a lot more fun with a few laughs along the way.

Leading off the launch, we have *USA TODAY* bestselling author Millie Criswell with *Staying Single*. This heroine is determined to remain single—three almost weddings is enough for one girl, isn't it?—no matter what her marriage-focused mother says. But after meeting a certain photojournalist, she just might have second thoughts....

Rounding out the month is Stephanie Doyle's *One True Love?* Believing that each person has only one true love, our heroine is in a bit of a dilemma. Turns out that the guy she picked isn't the same guy who's captured her thoughts. This calls for some rearranging...fast!

Look for two Harlequin Flipside books every month at your favorite bookstore. And check us out online at www.HarlequinFlipside.com. We hope you enjoy this new line of romantic comedy stories.

See you next month!

Wanda Ottewell
Editor

Mary-Theresa Hussey
Executive Editor

IT WAS A BAD DAY for a wedding.

Francie Morelli gazed down the red-carpeted aisle toward the altar, where her handsome husband-to-be, Matt Carson, all smiles and nervous perspiration in a black Armani tux, awaited her arrival, and knew this with a certainty.

Though unlike Matt, Francie wasn't nervous, just panicked. The kind of panic you get when you can't catch your breath or feel as though you might throw up.

Okay, so maybe she was a teensy bit nervous.

Even though she'd done the wedding thing twice before and knew what to expect. Not that she had ever actually made it all the way to the altar and said her "I dos."

Not that she would get that far this time, either.

Swallowing with some difficulty at the dangerous thoughts going through her mind, she tried to ignore the "Run, Francie, run!" mantra currently playing to the tune of "Burn, Baby, Burn" from *Disco Inferno,* the song so popular in the 70s.

The choice of music was a bad omen. Burning in hell was a likely possibility if she didn't go through with this wedding, which was probably the lesser of the two evils, because she knew Josephine Morelli's punishment would be far worse. Traveling on her mother's guilt trips was like taking a go-cart tour of hell.

Through her blush veil—flapping like a leaf in high wind due to her labored breathing—she could see her mother, dressed in a lovely, silk, teal-blue dress, hands locked in prayer and supplication, pleading with the Almighty to let her daughter have the courage to go through with the ceremony this time. The older woman's tear-filled eyes—Francie knew there were tears because her mother liked to make a good showing at public events (funerals were her specialty)—were fixed on the massive gold crucifix hanging above the altar, as if by sheer will alone she could command God to do her bidding, as Josephine had commanded Francie so many times before.

Fortunately for the world at large, God seemed to have a stronger backbone than Francie.

A hushed silence surrounded her as those in attendance waited to see if she would actually go through with the ceremony. Aunt Flo was biting her nails to the quick, while Grandma Abrizzi had her rosary beads clacking at top speed. No one could recite the rosary faster than Loretta Abrizzi, who was a definite contender for the *Guinness Book of World Records.*

Francie's sixteen-year-old brother, Jack, had taken perverse delight in explaining that several of the male guests, her uncles in particular, had placed bets on the outcome of today's event. The odds were five-to-one that she would never see her wedding night.

Ha! A lot they knew!

She'd already had several wedding nights, though she hadn't bothered with the *wedding* part. She likened it to eating dessert before dinner—the yum without the humdrum.

Not that Francie had anything in particular against matrimony. It just wasn't right for her. She had no desire to become an extension of a man and to cater to his whims.

Though Josephine was a strong woman, who came across as an independent sort, the woman lived for her children and husband. And even though John Morelli was a great guy and a terrific father, he liked things just so—like dinner on the table promptly at five o'clock every evening, his boxers ironed without creases and no interruptions during his weekly poker game with the guys.

Of course, Francie had a theory about her mother's catering to her family's needs. It was Josephine's way to control, to retain the upper hand with her husband and children, and she did it extremely well. Just as she had turned meddling into an art form.

Meddling, like marriage, was another one of those M-words that Francie hated: meddling, marriage, menstruation, menopause, milk of magnesia—Josephine's remedy for every childhood ailment—and last but not least, Matt, the last in a long line of M fiancés.

No. M-words were definitely not good. She'd have to remember that the next time she dated, if there was a next time. At the moment that seemed remote...redundant...and oh, so ridiculous.

She would not allow her mother to bully her again.

Period.

Standing beside Francie, John Morelli clutched his daughter's arm in a death grip, trying to keep her steady and on course. But Francie knew, just as he did, that it wouldn't. She was in collision mode and there was no way to avoid it.

Still, he had to try. His wife would expect no less. And John, like most of the Morellis, wasn't going to buck Josephine's wedding obsession. Not if he wanted a moment's peace.

Josephine was in no way, shape or form a passive-aggressive personality. The outspoken woman just came out and told you exactly what she thought and what she expected you to do about it. There was never a moment's doubt where you stood with the overbearing woman, lovingly nicknamed "The Terminator" by her three children.

It wasn't that the Morelli kids didn't love their mother; they did. It was just that Josephine was not an easy woman to deal with. Forget about living with her!

Francie's toes began to tingle—a surefire indication that flight was imminent. She wiggled them, hoping and praying that the urge to flee would pass. If not, the white satin shoes she wore would, like Dorothy's ruby slippers, whisk her away from the solemn occasion to her favorite place of refuge: Manny's Little Italy Deli. There she knew the owner, former high school classmate, Manny Delisio, would be waiting for her with a pastrami on rye and a large diet Coke.

Okay, so stress made her hungry!

Her roommate, Leo Bergmann, suitably armed

with a packed suitcase and a train ticket to an as-yet-unknown destination, would also be there to offer moral support and a stern lecture. He was almost as good as Josephine when it came to offering opinions and advice that no one wanted, only he did it with a bit more finesse.

Francie and Leo had agreed that if it looked as though she was going to bolt, Leo would leave the ceremony early, head down to Manny's and proceed with the travel arrangements he'd previously put into motion.

The last time Francie had run, Leo had chosen New York City as her escape destination. A great choice, in her opinion, for she'd been able to lose herself among the throngs of people, become invisible, and get her head back on straight before returning to face the music—translation: Josephine's ranting about what an ungrateful daughter she had.

Unfortunately the time before that—the first time, when Francie had fled the arms of the unfortunate Marty Ragusa, "Philadelphia's only undertaker with panache," as he called himself on those stupid TV commercials he appeared in—Leo had picked Pittsburgh. It hadn't been far enough away from Philadelphia or her mother, who had tracked her down like a bloodhound with a nose bent on revenge.

Josephine's anger had given new meaning to the term "pissed off." Though Francie wasn't entirely certain that her mother hadn't been more upset about losing her discount on funerals and burial plots than losing Marty for a son-in-law.

Patting his daughter's hand reassuringly, John

leaned over and smiled lovingly. The scent of Old Spice washed over Francie, conjuring up many good childhood memories, including her dad pushing her on the backyard swing or helping with division and multiplication problems.

"Don't be nervous, *cara mia*. Soon this will be over and you'll be married and settled down. It's the right thing to do, you'll see. And it will make your mother very happy. You know how she's waited for this day."

The second coming paled by comparison!

Francie adored her father and wanted to agree with him; she wanted that more than anything. But words of reassurance stuck in her throat like oversize peanuts and all she could offer up was a gaseous smile and a deer-in-the-headlights look.

Behind her, red-haired Joyce Rialto, her best friend since first grade, muttered, "Uh-oh," and then began cursing obscenities beneath her breath.

Joyce knew Francie a little too well, unfortunately.

"I'm sorry, Pop, but I don't think I can go through with this. I'm just not ready to get married. I'm not sure I'll ever be ready."

John's eyes widened momentarily, then he looked down the long aisle to where his wife was sitting in the first pew, the smile on her face suddenly melting as she noticed his resigned, worried expression.

"Your car's out back. I gassed it up, just in case, and left some money in the glove box."

Joyce wasn't the only one who knew her well.

Warmed by the gesture, Francie kissed her father's

cheek. "I love you, Pop. Thanks! I hope Ma doesn't give you too bad a time of it."

John glanced quickly at his wife again and groaned inwardly, noting that her frown had deepened and she was staring daggers at him. "Don't kiss me again! Your mother will think I'm in on this, and then there'll be hell to pay. Now go, if you're going. I'll handle your mother. I've been doing it for thirty-five years, haven't I?"

Francie knew her father spoke with more bravado than he felt. It wasn't that her dad was a coward; it was just that...well, he was married to Josephine.

"Yes, and you're still relatively sane. I love you!"

Despite his warning, she kissed him again, then turned and, with an apologetic smile at Joyce, her younger sister, Lisa, who was grinning widely at her, and the other two bridesmaids, who merely groaned before waving and wishing her good luck, hightailed it out of the church and into the warm September sunshine.

MARK FIELDING was late.

He should have been at St. Mary's Catholic Church twenty-five minutes ago for his stepbrother's wedding to perform his duties as best man. Matt was counting on him.

But his flight from the Philippines, where he'd been on assignment as a photojournalist with the Associated Press for the past six months, had been delayed, and the traffic on Interstate 95 from the airport into the city had been horrific. And to complicate matters, his cell phone wasn't working. Mark cursed his stupidity in not remembering to recharge the battery, though lack of sleep had played a significant role in rendering him temporarily stupid.

Spotting the brick church up ahead, he looked for a place large enough to park his SUV and shook his head at the impossibility of the situation. As he did, the heavy walnut doors to the church flew open and a woman dressed in full bridal regalia, veil blowing back to reveal dark hair and a very pretty face, ran out and down the steps.

This had to be his new sister-in-law.

What was her name? Frances? Fiona? Florence?

Applying the brake, he reached out to grab the camera on the seat next to him, rolled down the window and began snapping photos, while he recited all the F names he knew.

For the life of him, Mark couldn't remember her name. He'd never met his little brother's fiancée and hadn't been enamored of the idea that Matt was getting married so quickly after meeting the woman just three short months ago.

Hell, he knew dogs who'd had longer courtships!

And what was that saying? Marry in haste...

"Shit! I'm too late. I missed the wedding. They're already married."

A thousand apologies raced through his mind until the realization hit him that his brother hadn't followed his bride out of the church, nor had any of the relatives, including his dad and stepmother. They should have been waiting on the church steps to greet the happy couple with rice or birdseed or whatever the hell it was that folks used these days to pelt happy couples all in the name of good luck.

Setting the camera aside, he double-parked his green Ford Explorer and watched his brother's new bride lift her wedding dress off the ground, displaying a pair of rather nice legs, then disappear around the side of the church, looking over her shoulder a few times as if to make sure no one was following.

Why was the bride so anxious to leave?

And where the hell was his brother?

Suddenly, Mark got a really bad feeling in the pit of his stomach that had nothing to do with the dry turkey sandwich he'd eaten on the plane a few hours before. He made it a point to always heed his gut instincts; they'd never steered him wrong in the past.

And Mark knew his brother to be the sensitive sort, who wore his heart on his sleeve and romanticized every little thing about his relationships. Hadn't he warned Matt that wearing rose-colored glasses would get him into trouble one day?

Marry in haste...repent at leisure.

He'd been the romantic once, before he'd woken up to the fact that women of today weren't interested in commitment or long-term relationships, and that they didn't know their own minds.

It was slam, bam, thank you, mister!

Mark's recent relationships had left him unfulfilled. The sex had been great. But sex without commitment was just...well, sex.

He wanted more than that. He wanted what his parents had—love, trust, someone to share a life with.

But all he'd gotten so far was a swift kick in the butt

and feeble explanations of the "I'm not ready to commit yet" sort. Mark was all kinds of a fool to even think he'd meet anyone interested in making a life with him.

Women, he'd discovered the hard way, were duplicitous, selfish and self-serving. And he was damn sick and tired of it. So much so that if he found out that his brother's new bride was of a similar ilk, there was going to be hell to pay. He'd make damn sure of that.

"YOU NAUGHTY GIRL! I had a sick feeling that something would go wrong today. Of course, I base that on three years of living with you. Cold feet again, huh?"

Leo's familiar face warmed Francie's heart as she ripped off her veil, pulled aside the voluminous folds of white organza and lace that made up the skirt of her wedding gown and sat next to him at the small round table, waving and smiling at Manny, who was across the deli preparing a customer's order.

"Hey, Francie!" Manny called. "What's this one make? Number three, right? And you call your mother The Terminator." He threw back his head and laughed, then added, "I'm just glad I got over my crush on you when I was seventeen, or I'd have ended up a ruined man."

Francie smiled weakly. "You got my pastrami on rye ready? I can't stick around here long. My mother will be on my trail in no time."

"Leo's got everything. I'm just finishing up his take-out order. It'll be just a few more minutes."

Francie's roommate reached out and clasped her

hand, his touch as comforting as always. Next to Joyce, Leo was her best friend. Not only did they share an apartment, they shared confidences, relationship problems and Leo's obsession with dining out.

"Tell me what happened, sweetie. I really thought Matt had a chance. He's just so adorable. But I digress. Apparently you don't find him as attractive as I do." He grinned and the cleft in his chin dimpled.

Heaving a sigh, Francie replied, "Matt's wonderful. I like him a lot. He's handsome, successful—a great guy. But I don't love him, and that's the problem. I'm just not ready to take that final step. I don't want to spend the rest of my life with someone I don't love."

If she ever decided to get married—and that was a big *if*, and not at all likely, especially after today—she wanted to find a man who would knock her socks off, sweep her off her feet and make her fall madly in love. Since no such man existed, on this planet anyway, Francie felt relatively safe from the strangulation...um, *bonds* of matrimony.

"I take it there was no spark between you two."

"His kisses were nice, but..." She shook her head, wondering if her expectations were too high. Maybe those tingles, that quickening of the heartbeat and sweaty palms she'd been reading about didn't really exist.

"Bells and whistles didn't go off?"

"Exactly. I'm just glad Matt was willing to wait to consummate our relationship. I sort of insisted we delay until the honeymoon and..."

Leo's grin was lascivious. "Hey, maybe he's gay."

"You're incorrigible, Leo. Matt seems very straight to me. He's just a nice guy, who made the mistake of falling in love with the wrong woman...namely me. And now I've hurt him terribly, and I hate myself for it.

"I should have never let my mother browbeat me into marriage. This obsession she has about me getting married is unhealthy...for both of us."

Josephine's greatest aspiration in life was to see her two daughters married and settled down, preferably with five or six children that she could dote on, but she'd take two if push came to shove.

Her mother had spent years saving for Francie's wedding—now weddings—making elaborate plans, buying not one, but three fabulous dresses, finding not one, but three *perfect*, in her estimation, grooms. And knowing how much all this meant to her mother, Francie had a difficult time bursting her bubble.

Did she say Josephine had turned meddling into an art form? Try manipulation. She was even better at that.

"So, just say no."

Francie rolled her eyes at the absurdity of Leo's suggestion. "Have you ever tried saying no to my mother? Josephine is like a steamroller, leveling everything in her path. She never gives up, just keeps at me until all I want her to do is shut up and leave me alone. In the end I always relent, and she knows it. I've done it all my life. I'm programmed for it. Twenty-nine years old, and I'm pathetic."

Nodding in understanding, Leo squeezed her hand

gently. "I know, sweetie. But there's going to come a day when you'll have to stand up to Josephine. I think if you do, she'll back down."

"Really?" A tiny kernel of hope blossomed in Francie's chest, reflecting in her voice. "Do you think so, Leo?"

Apology filling his dark eyes, he shook his head. "No. But it sounds like good advice. You can't keep allowing your mother to control your life, Francie. These trips to the altar are not only emotionally taxing, they're expensive."

She sighed at the truth of his words, knowing her job with Ted Baxter Promotions didn't pay that well. Not enough to keep up with recent expenditures, anyway. "Where am I going this time?"

"Niagara Falls. I thought there was a nice irony to it."

Her eyes widened in disbelief. "Niagara F... You're kidding, right? I'll be hanging out with honeymooners, couples making cooing noises at each other. I may have to throw up."

"It was the cheapest destination I could find. Your Visa is about maxed out, thanks to all that junk you purchased for your honeymoon."

"It was expensive lingerie, not junk. And that just goes to show you that I had every intention of going through with the wedding. I never set out to hurt Matt and ruin his life, not to mention my own."

"He'll get over it. They all do. Marty Ragusa is marrying a former Victoria's Secret model, so I think his heart has mended."

"That's good. I'm happy to hear it." And relieved.

It lessened the guilt she felt a wee bit. "I'm not sure Michael Maxwell has fared as well. Last I heard the poor man was wandering the Australian Outback, trying to find himself."

"He'll probably find a kangaroo instead, which will match his personality to a T. What you saw in that bozo is beyond me. The man was dull, dull, dull."

Francie shook her head and sighed. "I'm a terrible person, Leo. I've hurt so many people."

"Not terrible, sweetie, just spineless. You'll do better the next time."

She shook her head adamantly, and with a mutinous expression plastered on her face, said, "I'm not doing this again! I will never let my mother push me into another marriage. I have *almost* married for the last time. I've decided to remain a bachelorette. I'll date, have sex, just enjoy the hell out of my life, but I'm never going to walk down the aisle again."

No more engagements. No more weddings. *No way!*

2

IT WAS THE MOST depressing wedding reception Mark had ever attended, and he'd been to some strange ones in his thirty-four years.

Of course, unhappiness tended to set in when there was no bride in attendance.

But Steve and Laura Fielding had decided that since the reception at the Hyatt Regency was already paid for, thirty pounds of fresh shrimp stood to go to waste—not to mention massive amounts of liquor— and Matt hadn't wanted to disappoint his high school and college buddies, many of whom had traveled great distances to be with him on his special day, the reception would go on as planned.

Mark's stepmom had always been a practical woman—practical, loving and wise. After his mother had died in a tragic car accident, Mark had lucked out the day his father had found such a wonderful woman to marry and to make a new life with.

Mark had been four years old at the time of Helena Fielding's death, and six by the time his dad had re-married his former secretary, Laura Carson. And he had never felt anything but love and kindness from the pretty petite blonde.

Laura had stepped into her role as his mother with

enthusiasm and caring, giving Mark all the love and attention he craved. And even though she had a son of her own, two years his junior by a previous marriage, Mark had never felt slighted or the need to compete with his stepbrother. In fact, he and Matt were as close as or closer than brothers who'd been delivered from the same womb.

Spotting his brother seated at a table across the large ballroom, the lights of the crystal chandelier glittering down upon him, illuminating his cheerless expression, Mark moved to join him.

Sympathetic friends and family had surrounded Matt all evening, making it impossible for Mark to have a serious discussion about the flighty woman in white satin who'd deserted his little brother.

Trisha Yearwood's version of "How Will I Live?" blared from the DJ's oversize speakers, and Mark thought it a fitting tune for the occasion—maudlin without being overly sickening.

Pulling out a chair, he sat. "I'm sorry as hell about all this, Matt, but I guess you already know that."

Matt, who'd already consumed four beers and was halfway through his fifth, looked up and nodded, his slightly crooked smile sad. "I never saw it coming, Mark. It was love at first sight, a whirlwind courtship. Francie seemed so perfect for me. I thought for sure that she loved me as much as I loved her." He heaved a deep sigh. "Guess I was wrong."

Noting the hurt in his brother's eyes, the slump to his shoulders, Mark cursed softly under his breath, wishing he had Francesca Morelli in front of him at that moment.

Didn't the woman have a conscience?

Didn't the selfish bitch know how much she had hurt Matt?

Didn't she care?

Obviously the answer was *no*, on all three counts.

Grabbing one of the Bud Lights, he popped it open and downed the liquid in one gulp. "I haven't had much luck with women, bro. I find them to be heartless creatures with a phobia to commit."

"You're probably right. Francie's run before. A mutual friend told me that she'd left her two previous fiancés at the altar. Even so, I never expected it to happen to me. Guess I was stupid to think it'd be different this time."

Mark's look was incredulous. His brother was even more naive than he thought. "You knew this about the woman and still you wanted to marry her? Unbelievable."

"I loved her. Still do, as a matter of fact. Love is funny like that. It blinds you to people's flaws, makes you do crazy things. You've never been in love, so you wouldn't know what I'm talking about, Mark."

Wrong! Mark knew in spades. He'd been in love once, with the faithless Nicole Gordon. The woman had cheated on him, lied about it, ripped out his heart and stomped all over it with her four-inch heels, then married the bastard with whom she'd been having the affair.

Mark knew all he wanted to know about women.

"You shouldn't have rushed into marriage, Matt. Three months is not long enough to get to know someone you intend to spend the rest of your life with."

"You're not trying to give me advice, are you?" Matt shook his head. "Not with your track record and failure rate? Unfriggingbelievable."

"Touché. But you looked like you needed some advice and cheering up, so here I am." Grinning, Mark knocked his brother on the arm. "Come on, bro. Buck up. You dodged a bullet today, if you ask me. Obviously this Francie isn't in her right mind if she's willing to give up a great guy like you. And what do you really know about her?"

"She comes from a large Italian family. Josephine and John Morelli are nice people, though the mother is a bit controlling."

"I take it Josephine was the harridan in the blue dress that kept screaming and wailing that this couldn't be happening again, then crossing herself in front of the altar and vowing revenge?"

Matt finally smiled. "That's the one. Josephine's a bit high-strung. She drives Francie nuts. I admit I was a bit apprehensive about having her for a mother-in-law, but Francie assured me that her mom's bark is worse than her bite, which is good, because the woman seemed a bit rabid at times."

"I take it Francie doesn't live with her parents, then?"

"She's got an apartment near Rittenhouse Square. Lives with some guy named Leo Bergmann. He has money, apparently."

Mark's brow lifted. "Maybe he's the reason she's

hesitant to wed. Maybe they've got something going."

"I've met Leo. He's a really nice guy, but women aren't his thing, if you get my drift."

"Gotcha. So, what does Francie do for a living? Does she have a job?"

"She works at a small public relations firm downtown."

"Which one?"

Matt's brow wrinkled in confusion. "Why are you asking so many questions about Francie? It's a bit moot at this point, don't you think? It's over. I only allow myself one public humiliation in a lifetime."

Sipping his beer, Mark tried to look nonchalant. He had his reasons for asking the probing questions. If he had anything to say about it—and he was pretty sure he did—Francie Morelli had dumped her last groom.

Of course, he didn't intend to let his lovesick brother in on his plan, which was just starting to take shape.

It was time someone taught this Morelli woman a lesson, gave her a bit of her own medicine, so she could experience just how rotten it was to play with other people's emotions and lives.

At the moment he wasn't sure how, but he intended to extract a pound of flesh for what his brother had gone through.

An eye for an eye. A wedding for a wedding. A bride for a groom.

THE DOORBELL BUZZED three times and Francie froze, a sick feeling forming in the pit of her stomach.

"Please, God, don't let it be my mother!"

Her mother knew, by osmosis, voodoo or tarot readings that Francie was back in town. How she knew, Francie wasn't certain. The woman had a sixth sense when it came to her children, and Francie lived in fear that Josephine was standing on the other side of her apartment door, waiting to pounce.

"Francie, it's me. Open up. I know you're in there."

Releasing the breath she was holding, Francie unlocked the door to find her sister in mid-knock. Lisa was wearing jeans and a red T-shirt, her long black hair pulled back in a ponytail. She looked understated and chic. Not that Lisa would care. Her sister wasn't into fashion. And she had no idea how attractive she was, which was a big part of her charm.

Smiling smugly, Lisa, all one hundred and ten pounds of her, pushed her way in with the same determination as a three-hundred-pound linebacker. "Thought it was Ma, huh? Well, that's what you get for sneaking out of town and letting the rest of us take the heat. Dealing with The Terminator wasn't pretty, I can tell you that. This past week has been pure hell. It's a wonder Dad still has his hearing. I had no idea that Mom's vocabulary had grown so much. She used curse words that even I've never heard of."

Francie sighed. "Sorry to put you and Dad through that, but I've had my own week of hell."

"Oh, well, that makes me feel a bit better then. *Not!*" Lisa plopped down on the red leather sofa studded with brass tacks and reached for the bowl of toffee peanuts Leo always left on the coffee table.

Lisa ate like a pig and never gained an ounce: Francie thought it was extremely unfair. She had cellulite in places she didn't want to think about.

"How come your week was so bad?" Lisa asked between munches.

"Niagara Falls. Need I say more?"

Her sister burst out laughing, nearly choking on a nut in the process. "Leo's got a great sense of humor, I'll give him that. Got any diet Coke? These nuts are making me thirsty."

"In the fridge. And I don't see anything remotely funny about it," Francie called after her sister, who had headed off to the kitchen in search of a soda. "I didn't laugh the entire time I was there." Though she did a great deal of crying and soul-searching.

Being surrounded by happy, loving couples had been torturous for Francie, who didn't believe she would ever marry someone she loved, much less make it to the honeymoon portion. Not that she wanted to. But still...

She'd had three opportunities and blown them all—the opportunities, not the...

Whatever!

And she still had mixed feelings about the matrimonial state. The idea of living the rest of her life alone was depressing, but not enough to make her want to saddle herself to some man just for the sake of companionship or, God forbid, to make her mother happy.

Not that such a thing was possible!

Josephine rained down gloom and doom wherever she went and could always find the negative in any given situation.

At any rate, Francie thought, staying single wasn't the worst thing that could happen. She still had her health, friends...a good job.

Oh, God! She was starting to sound like her mother!

Shoot me now!

So what if she never met Mr. Right or had children?

The whole marriage and family thing was entirely overrated. She knew hype when she heard it. Since working in publicity and promotion, she could B.S. with the best of them.

And twenty-nine wasn't exactly spinsterish.

Okay, so Aunt Flo wasn't married and had turned into a miserable shrew, which was a nice way of saying that the woman was a raving bitch.

But that didn't mean anything.

Aunt Flo probably hadn't had sex in a billion years, which no doubt accounted for her sour disposition. And she had that knuckle-cracking thing going against her.

Francie's dry spell had been long, but not *that* long.

"I leave you alone for two minutes and you look like you've lost your best friend. What's wrong?" Lisa handed Francie a soda, then sat back down on the sofa. "I'm all ears, if you care to share the ugly details."

Francie heaved a dispirited sigh. "My life's a mess, Lisa. I've ruined three relationships and hurt some very nice men in the process. I'm confused about what it is I want from life, mad at Mom for putting me in this situation, over and over again, and I've gained three pounds. I'm miserable, not to mention, bloated."

"So you're a bitch. Get over it." Grinning at Francie's blossoming outrage, Lisa added, "Just kidding." Stuffing a throw pillow behind her head, she reclined on the sofa, not bothering to remove her shoes.

Where Francie was a neatnik, Lisa was somewhat of a slob. Sharing a bedroom with her as a teenager had been a nightmare. Francie had never known where candy wrappers and soda cans were going to show up.

"First of all, those men entered into their relationships with eyes wide open," Lisa went on. "Okay, maybe not the undertaker, since he was the first victim, er, I mean, prospective groom, but the other two knew of your penchant for running and they still proposed.

"You're no Julia Roberts, but you have given her a bit of competition as the *Runaway Bride*.

"Second, Mom is never going to change, so you need to stand up to her or accept that she's going to meddle. And you wear a size ten, so I'm not at all sorry for you."

Easy to say from someone who wore a six, Francie thought.

"And finally, I hope you do get married one of these days because then Mom will get off my back."

"Don't count on it."

"Isn't that the truth? I was looking through her dresser drawer for a scarf the other day and found a list of prospective grooms she'd been making for me." Lisa made a face, then a gagging noise. "Alan

Swarski was on the list. Can you imagine? *Alan Swarski!* The man is almost sixty and has grandchildren. What can she be thinking? He has nose hair, not to mention a gut, for chrissake! What am I, desperate? I do have some pride, after all."

"If he's breathing, he's an eligible candidate."

The front door opened and Leo strolled in carrying a white bakery bag. He smiled widely when he spotted Lisa. "Hey, girl! You're looking good. I bought bagels and cream cheese, if you're hungry." He held up the bag and the enticing aroma of freshly baked bagels clouded the room.

Francie's stomach rumbled. "I am. Hand them over."

"Bagels." Lisa's face fell. "I was hoping for a ham sandwich."

"On Sunday morning? I always buy bagels for Francie and me on Sunday. It's tradition. And since she just got home late last night I figured she'd need refueling before facing your mother."

He turned to Francie, a worried look on his face—though not as worried as Francie's—and handed her the bag. "Has Josephine called?"

Francie shook her head. "Not yet. Ma's got a bar mitzvah this afternoon that's been on her schedule for weeks. That'll keep her busy for a while. She'll be mentally calculating all the money the Goldstein kid receives, then comparing it to the other bar mitzvahs she's attended to see how the Goldsteins stack up in popularity."

Popularity in her parents' neighborhood was often gauged by the amount of money that was taken in at religious events such as weddings, christenings and bar mitzvahs. And God forbid if small flower arrangements or a poor showing at a viewing occurred during a funeral. You might as well pack up and leave town in that case, for it meant you were persona non grata.

Francie didn't fully understand the hierarchy, rules and social strata that comprised an ethnic neighborhood, but she knew they existed.

"You're only postponing the inevitable, Francie. You know that, don't you?" Leo leveled a disappointed look at her. "At some point you've got to face your mother. Now is as good a time as any."

Lisa, having noted Francie's horrified expression, quickly changed the subject, much to Francie's great relief.

"So, who's your latest love interest, Leo?" Lisa asked in her usual tactless manner.

Francie knew her sister was not known for her finesse. In fact, Lisa was enough like Josephine to be scary.

"I saw you at Club Zero last night," she went on. "The guy you were with was cute. To tell you the truth, it made me rather jealous. There aren't enough men out there, as it is. Damn shame all the good ones are either married or gay."

The blond man, who resembled a young Elton John, grinned. "I'm taking that as a compliment, sweetie. Phillip's his name and he's an architect. We exchanged phone numbers. Nothing more."

"Well, that's better than I did. Molly and I struck out. No wonder they call the place Club *Zero*."

"Consider yourself lucky," Francie said. "Men, present company excepted, are more trouble than they're worth. You're better off alone."

Lisa rolled her eyes. "I don't want to get married. I just want to get laid. It's been so long I'm going to forget how to do it. And don't tell me it's like riding a bike. Even bike parts rust."

"Why didn't you just ask some guy for his phone number?" Leo took a seat on an overstuffed chair. "This is the new millennium. You're entitled."

"Quit trying to lead my baby sister astray, Leo. I don't want her hooking up with a serial rapist."

"Ha!" Francie's sister rolled her eyes. "Fat chance of that happening. I usually attract serial geeks, not rapists."

The phone rang and everyone froze, staring at it as if it were an evil entity out to do them harm.

"It's Mom," Lisa said.

Shaking her head, Francie took several steps back, wishing she had a string of garlic around her neck, or at the very least, a gold crucifix. "I'm not taking her call. Tell Mom I died, that I fell over the falls. Tell her anything, but don't tell her I'm here."

"Coward," Leo said, reaching for the portable phone. "Oh, hello, Mrs. Morelli. Yes, Francie's right here. Hold on. I'll get her for you."

"Bastard!" Francie took the phone from Leo's hand, none too gently, and shook it at him. "I'll get you for this."

Lisa popped more nuts into her mouth and, like any good sibling, enjoyed watching her sister squirm.

Francie prayed that the floor beneath her feet

would open up and swallow her whole. A trip straight to hell would be preferable to explaining to Josephine why wedding number three had been a no go.

3

TWO WEEKS AFTER what Mark always thought of as the "wedding from hell," he stood outside the offices of Ted Baxter Promotions and adjusted his red silk tie.

Normally he didn't wear suits and ties—he didn't need to dress up in his profession—preferring jeans and T-shirts or sweatshirts.

But today was special.

Today he intended to put his plan into motion for seducing Francesca Morelli.

With a nod of thanks to the young, dewy-eyed blond receptionist, he entered the inner office to find the surroundings not nearly as attractive as the woman seated behind the massive oak desk.

She was wearing a red cashmere sweater set that hugged her firm breasts. On the ring finger of her left hand his brother's diamond-and-ruby engagement ring was noticeably absent, bringing his mind back to the matter at hand.

"May I help you?" she asked, looking up from the papers spread out in front of her and gathering them up into a neat little pile before pushing them to one side.

Gazing into the warmest, most beautiful brown

eyes he'd ever seen, Mark's jaw nearly dropped to his chest. Long lashes, full lips, high cheekbones and a pert little nose made up a very arresting, exotic face.

Damn! His brother's ex-fiancée was a knockout. He had thought that from a distance the day of the wedding, and the photos he'd taken had certainly proven that out, but seeing Francesca Morelli up close and personal cemented his earlier opinion.

And it was something he hadn't planned on.

"I'm Mark Fielding. I was hoping to see Mr. Baxter. I'd like to arrange a publicity campaign to promote my first book, but I haven't a clue how to go about it. I was hoping he might be able to help me out."

She smiled sweetly at him and he sucked in air. "I'm sorry, Mr. Fielding, but Ted... Mr. Baxter isn't here at the moment. Is there something I can help you with? Perhaps answer some questions? I often assist with clients when Mr. Baxter's out of the office."

Yeah, you can tell me why you dumped my brother.

And why you're so damned attractive.

Pasting on his most charming smile, he heard her sharp intake of breath. Her reaction pleased him, on more than one level, for it made what he had to do a whole lot easier. For some reason, women had always found him attractive. They just didn't want to have long-term relationships with him.

"I'm a photojournalist. My first book of photographs will be published next spring, and I thought it might be wise to do some pre-publicity and promotion for it. My publishing house isn't likely to shell out any money, since I'm new a new author. I figured if I want the book to succeed I'd better do it myself."

"That's very wise, Mr. Fielding. May I ask what made you choose Baxter Promotions? We're not a very large company and not widely known outside of the local area."

Mark had rehearsed what he intended to say, and the lie rolled easily off his tongue. "A friend of mine recommended it several months back. I believe you handled some public relations matters for his law firm."

She nodded. "That's entirely possible. We have many satisfied clients. Baxter Promotions is proud of its reputation in the community."

"Good to hear. There's nothing worse than bad word of mouth for a business such as yours."

Her eyes widened momentarily, then the phone buzzed and she excused herself to answer it. Apparently, Ms. Morelli was the only employee in the small firm, aside from the receptionist out front.

Francesca Morelli grinned at something the person on the other end of the line was saying and two charming dimples appeared; Mark's gut responded with nine bars of "Hot! Hot! Hot!"

Damn her for being so attractive!

And damn you for noticing, Fielding.

Francie Morelli was a tight little package. Nice boobs—not too big, yet not small, either. Her legs, he recalled, were quite shapely, and he supposed that if she stood, he'd find that her ass was equally as appealing as the rest of her.

Taking Ms. Morelli to bed and making love to her wasn't going to be much of a chore, that was for damn certain. Mark intended to enjoy every minute of it, before dumping Little Miss Fickle on that cute little ass and saying, *"Hasta la vista,* baby!"

"YOU BREAK a mother's heart, Francie. I don't know how you can treat me this way. Three times you have been to the altar in front of God, not to mention all of our relatives and friends, and three times you have disgraced me and your father." Josephine crossed herself and then murmured a little prayer, clearly hoping for a little intervention from on high.

Seating herself at the ancient red Formica table in her parents' kitchen, Francie sighed at the hurt flickering in her mother's dark eyes, then filled both of their cups with strong, hot coffee.

Josephine's coffee was so strong you could stand a spoon up in it. And coffee did seem to make bad news digest better, though chocolate was better, of course. But this morning wasn't a good time for chocolate. It wasn't a good time for conversation, either. But like Leo said, now was as good a time as any. Francie couldn't run from the truth indefinitely. She'd already tried that these past two weeks.

"Ma, I never wanted to hurt you or Dad. But you keep harping on me to get married and have babies, and I'm just not ready to take that step." Not that she'd ever be ready, but there was no sense in dashing all of Josephine's hopes in one fell swoop.

"What do you mean, you're not ready? You're twenty-nine, Francesca, practically an old maid."

Francie did her best not to wince.

"Your aunts talk behind my back about how you're never going to have a husband and children. And your sister is no better. She doesn't even date nice men. Soon they'll be saying that both of my daughters are lesbians." Josephine crossed herself again, on the off chance that it might be true.

Her mother tolerated Leo, but Francie didn't think for a minute that tolerance would extend to any of her children or family members should they choose an alternative lifestyle.

Francie was a tried and true—not to mention, proven—heterosexual woman, but she thought there was a lot to be said for the lesbian lifestyle.

First, if you were lucky enough to find another woman who wore the same size, you could expand your wardrobe. That couldn't happen with a man, unless you were built like a fullback. A woman didn't care about another woman's lack of makeup or weight gain. And they had oodles more experience when it came to knowing what women wanted in the sex department.

Some of the men Francie had dated hadn't known which end was up and could have benefited from a sex education class. Lesson One: Orgasms We Have Known and Loved.

"My heart is breaking from this, Francesca. I want to see you married and settled before I die. Is this too much to ask? I'm not getting any younger and neither are you."

"Before I die" was one of Josephine's favorite expressions. It was conjured up whenever guilt was needed to make her children toe the line. No matter that she was as healthy as the proverbial horse, in Josephine's mind death was imminent if she didn't get her way.

"Stop it, Ma! You're not going to die." *In the immortal words of Billy Joel, "Only the good die young."* Francie left that unsaid, however. Her mother had never been a Billy Joel fan, preferring Placido Domingo instead.

"You can't keep trying to run—" *make that, ruin* "—my life. Yes, I'm twenty-nine years old. But I'm very happy being single. I don't need a man to complete me, and I'm not a lesbian."

Josephine seemed inordinately relieved by that admission.

"Someday maybe I'll meet someone." Mark Fielding's face flashed before her eyes, but Francie blinked it away, wondering why she suddenly thought of the handsome photographer, a man she hardly knew—a man who set her toes to tingling.

Sipping her coffee, she wished fervently for chocolate and issued a cease and desist order for her toes to stop misbehaving.

"But I'm not ready now. There are things I want to do with my life—travel, meet interesting people—" *men who worked for the Associated Press were definitely interesting* "—achieve success in my career. I'm just not ready to settle down."

Eyes raised heavenward, Josephine clenched her hands and shook them. "All meaningless things. Without a husband and children, a woman's life is nothing. Why would you want to work when you can find a good man to take care of you? You women of today don't make any sense at all."

"These are different times, Ma. Women don't need

to be married to feel fulfilled. You're happy doing for Dad, and that's great. But it's not what I want.

"Didn't you ever just want things for yourself, without thinking about how it would affect other people? I know it sounds selfish, and maybe it is, but so what? Since when did it become a crime to want independence? It's what this country was founded on."

Josephine stirred more sugar into her cup. The spoon hit the sides, clanking and clanking as she formed her answer. "I would not have done anything to disappoint my mother and father. It was expected that I marry, and I did. In my day children were dutiful."

In your day women were orgasm-less.

"But what about falling head over heels in love?"

Looking somewhat insulted, her mother sat back in her chair, her mouth opening and closing like a floundering fish. "I love your father. Don't talk crazy. You young people have too many romantic notions in your head. You watch movies, read those romance books, and you think that is what real life is supposed to be. But it's not.

"Real life, a good life, is taking care of others, making sure your husband has clean underwear in his drawer and hot food on the table when he gets home tired from work. It's taking pride in your children's accomplishments, like when you made your first communion, or when Jackie pitched the no-hitter in Little League, remember?"

Francie did, and she smiled at the memory of how thrilled her parents were for her little brother. Her mother celebrated the event with a cake and a party for all of Jackie's friends. "You're the best, Ma. We kids couldn't have asked for a better, more caring mother. But you shouldn't expect any of us to lead the same life as you. That's not fair."

Josephine grunted her disapproval. "What's fair—growing old alone?"

"I've tried to be the daughter you want. I've gone along with these weddings, to make you happy. But it's making me very unhappy. Not to mention the poor grooms in question. I'm sure Matt Carson will never speak to me again. And I truly liked Matt, as a friend."

"His mother said there were no hard feelings. She's a lovely woman, that Mrs. Fielding. She would have made you a good mother-in-law."

A good mother-in-law! Now there was an oxymoron if ever she heard one.

"I agree. Laura is a lovely woman, and a very gracious one to have said that. I know the Fieldings spent a lot of money on the reception and I feel terrible about it. And that's just what I'm talking about. These weddings have hurt a lot of people, including you and Dad. Your savings account has got to be suffering. And you need that money for your retirement. Dad can't sell appliances forever."

In fact, her dad had been talking retirement for the past two years, but had never gotten around to it. She wondered now if it was because he couldn't afford to.

Francie's guilt multiplied.

"I have money put aside for such things, Francie, you know that. And I will make you another wedding when you come to your senses. An even nicer one. We'll pick out a new dress, make our own arrangements for the reception, hire a better caterer..."

Francie knew that her mother hadn't heard a word she'd said, and probably never would. It was useless arguing with the headstrong woman. But she could be just as stubborn as Josephine, now that her mind was made up to remain single.

Francie would not be coerced into another wedding. And nothing or no one would convince her otherwise.

"IT WAS NICE OF YOU to have lunch with me today, Ms. Morelli, especially on such short notice. I found after returning to my hotel yesterday afternoon that I still had a lot of questions that needed answering, being new, as I am, to the publishing and promotions game."

"That's understandable, Mr. Fielding."

Francie and Mark were seated at the City Tavern, the oldest dining establishment in Philadelphia, located down by the waterfront, and Francie wondered at her acceptance of the luncheon appointment.

Of course, it was a business lunch. And she wanted Mr. Fielding's business for the company. But still... She didn't like mixing business with pleasure, especially when that business was over six feet tall, had deep blue eyes and a face that could rival Pierce Brosnan's.

Mark Fielding was definitely eye candy.

Francie was definitely addicted to candy.

Francie needs candy like a hole in the head!

"I was happy to oblige," she went on. "Baxter Promotions prides itself on being a very hands-on company."

His right brow shot up and she felt her face heat at what her words implied.

Way to insert foot in mouth, Francie!

"Really? How interesting."

Ignoring his teasing grin, she said, "As I explained, our firm is a small one, so we're able to give our clients more individualized attention. Details are very important in this business, as you are certain to find out, no matter who you decide to sign with."

He smiled that devastatingly sexy smile again. It was a sin for a man to have such straight, white teeth. Francie had paid a fortune to have hers fixed. In fact, she was still paying the orthodontist, would probably be paying Dr. Rosenblat until the day she died, or needed dentures.

"I like the sound of that, Ms. Morelli, or can I call you Francesca, since there's a good possibility that we'll be working together? I hope you'll call me Mark."

"How did you know my—"

"The brass plate on your desk."

She nodded. "Ah, of course." Francie was dying to ask Mark about his last name. Though Matt's last name was Carson, his parents' last name had been Fielding, due to a divorce and remarriage in his family. He had never mentioned anything about having a brother.

Matt had made a habit out of surprising her with all sorts of things—romantic gifts, tickets to concerts she'd been dying to see—so when he refused to give her the name of his best man and had insisted on issuing the invitation himself, saying only that it was a big surprise and she would have to wait until the day of the wedding to find out, she didn't insist.

Most grown men were really just little boys at heart, and Matt had been no different.

At any rate, Fielding was a pretty common name in the Philadelphia area, so she wasn't going to start getting paranoid about every person she met with that moniker. And Mark Fielding didn't look a thing like Matt, who was at least three inches shorter and had brown curly hair, not black waves that tempted a woman's touch.

Stop it, Francie! This line of thinking is only going to get you into trouble, and you have plenty of that already.

Not to mention that Mark starts with the dreaded letter "M," Francie reminded herself.

What is it about M names anyway? First Marty, then Mike, Matt, and now Mark. She had a serious alphabet problem.

"Was it something I said?"

Her cheeks filled with color again. "Sorry. I have a bad habit of zoning out. And yes, you may call me Francesca or Francie, if you like, which is what most of my friends and family call me."

The waiter came to take their order. Francie decided on the crab cakes, which was the chef's special for the day, while Mark opted for scallops in white wine sauce. They shared a bottle of chardonnay.

"So what kind of media coverage can I expect, if I decide to sign with Baxter? I was hoping to get on some talk shows, maybe a few radio spots." Mark forked salad into his mouth as he spoke, and Francie had a difficult time concentrating on his words and not his lips.

"There'll be book signings, of course. And with your affiliation with the Associated Press, I don't see a problem getting the TV talk shows interested. From the little you've told me, your work sounds fascinating, not to mention topical."

"It can be. But it can also be heart-wrenching at times. There's a lot of poverty, death and disease in this world, and I've seen and photographed most of it."

Over their main course, Mark told her what he'd seen in Africa—the deaths from AIDS, the famine—and detailed many other atrocities he'd witnessed in the countries he'd visited and photographed.

"I admire your ability to be able to deal with such things. I don't think I could."

"It's been difficult at times," he confessed, sadness filling his eyes. "I've had the opportunity to photograph some of what's been going on in North Korea, and it sickens me. The children look like prisoners in a concentration camp. They're so undernourished and badly treated. I wish our government could do something about it."

"You talk with a great deal of passion, Mark. That will be an asset when you're interviewed."

"It's not just talk. I feel very passionate about my work. I'm passionate about a great many things, actually."

His gazed dropped to her lips and Francie reached

for her water glass, trying to quench the heat she suddenly felt between her legs.

What on earth was wrong with her? She'd just broken off her engagement, left her groom at the altar, and here she was affected by yet another man!

Not good, Francie. Definitely not good.

"Is there a problem? You look a little flushed."

She pasted on an innocent smile. "Why, no. I just think it's rather warm in here, don't you?"

"Not at all. I think it's perfect, as a matter of fact. Great food, a charming companion. What more can a man ask for?"

Think about work, Francie, she told herself. "What made you decide to become a photographer?"

"It was something I'd dabbled with in high school. Once I knew I was pretty good at it, there was no holding me back. I snapped photos of everything, almost drove my parents nuts."

Noting Mark was finished with his lunch, she asked, "How was your meal?"

"I enjoyed it very much. This restaurant was an excellent choice."

"Would you care for dessert? The pastry chef is very good here."

"No thanks. I need to stop by my new apartment, make sure the furnishings have been delivered as promised."

"You rented an apartment? Does that mean you're planning to stay on awhile? I thought Associated Press photographers were on the road a lot."

"We are. But I requested assignments closer to home. I'm a bit travel weary and like the idea of putting down roots for a while. With my seniority, it wasn't a problem."

"So, where's your new apartment?"

"It's called The Stones at Rittenhouse Square. Do you know of it?"

Francie's mouth fell open, and her eyes widened. "But...but that's where I live."

Mark smiled, his right brow shooting up. "Really? What a nice coincidence. I guess that means we'll be seeing a lot of each other, then. I hope so, anyway."

Warning bells clanged in her ears and red flags waved wildly in front of her eyes, but as she gazed into Mark Fielding's big blue eyes, so filled with promise and passion, Francie ignored them completely.

4

PUSHING the rented sofa to a position beneath the bay window that overlooked the park across the street, Mark stood back, hands on hips, and surveyed the room.

Depressing at best, he decided.

It didn't come anywhere close to his elegantly furnished room at the Ritz-Carlton. But hey, it was temporary. Which was good. Because if he had to spend any significant amount of time with the red-brocade sofa and green-velvet wing chairs he might have to commit himself to an asylum for the criminally design challenged.

This had been a last-minute arrangement, so he couldn't afford to be too picky. Plus, it accomplished an important goal—living in close proximity to Francesca Morelli. *Beggars can't be choosers*, his stepmom always counseled, and she was usually right.

As if conjured up by his thoughts, the cell phone rang, and it was Laura on the other end. "Mark, are you okay? We haven't heard from you in days."

It had only been two, but he knew his mom was a worrier. "I'm fine, Mom. How're you doing? Hope you and Dad have recovered from the wedding." He knew they'd been exhausted by the ordeal, both physically and mentally.

Francie had a lot to atone for.

"You don't sound like you're in Afghanistan, Mark. If I didn't know better I'd think you were just a few blocks away. Very impressive technology. How do they do it?"

Mark felt heat rising up his neck at the lies he'd told his parents and brother. But it was a necessary fabrication if he was going to pull off his scheme. Matt was still too smitten with Francesca to be included in his plan for revenge. He'd have to go this one alone.

"Yeah, these digital cell phones work great, don't they? So how's Dad? And Mark? He was pretty depressed the last time I spoke to him. Is he doing any better since the wedding?"

"Not really." There was a great deal of worry in those two words. "That's why I'm calling, dear. Your father and I have decided to take a trip to Maui, and we've convinced Matt to go with us. I think the change of scenery will be good for him. For all of us, actually. We liked Francie very much, and this has been a difficult situation to deal with."

"I totally agree," he replied, trying to keep the anger he felt out of his voice. "When do you leave?"

"First thing tomorrow morning. Because of our last-minute booking it's costing us a small fortune for the plane tickets and hotel. But your dad thought it a necessary and worthwhile expense, so we're going. I wanted to let you know, in case you tried to call. I didn't want you to worry that something had happened to us."

Laura was like that, always so considerate of others—a total opposite to his brother's self-centered ex-fiancée. Oh sure, Francie came across as nice, because she wanted his business. But he knew what the woman was really like—a heartbreaker, ball-buster, selfish to the bone. She was no different from all the other women he'd known.

"I'm glad you called to let me know. Tell Matt I said to have a good time, and you do the same. You and Dad never really had a honeymoon, so make the most of this trip. Maui is a very romantic place. Try to relax and enjoy yourself."

Laura's embarrassed laughter filled his ears, making Mark smile. It was such fun to tease her. Because of his stepmom's fair complexion, her face always turned beet red whenever she got self-conscious about something.

"Always the romantic, son. It's one of the things I love best about you."

"Only one? When I have so many wonderful qualities," he quipped.

A knock sounded on the door just then, and Mark cursed softly under his breath, hoping his mother didn't grow suspicious.

"Did I just hear a knock, Mark? Where on earth are you?"

He thought quickly. "Ah, yeah, Mom. I ordered room service. This hotel is the pits, so I don't want to keep the guy waiting. He might decide to spit in my food. They're not real fond of Americans here."

"I understand. Call us when you can. And please

be careful. Your dad and I worry about you when you're over in those dangerous places."

Mark reassured her he would, then clicked off to answer the door, where he found a handsome blond man with a wiry build standing on the other side.

His visitor was impeccably dressed in a very expensive suit—Armani would be his guess—and he was holding a bottle of wine, which Mark accepted from his outstretched hand with a thank-you.

"I'm Leo Bergmann, Mark. Francie told me you were new to the building, so I've come by to welcome you. We're mostly a friendly group, except for Mrs. Hunsaker three doors down," he said, indicating the hallway to his right. "She's got inflamed hemorrhoids. A real nightmare, that woman. I'd try to stay clear of her, if I were you. There's not enough Preparation H in the entire world to cure what ails her. She gives new meaning to the term 'a pain in the ass.'"

Mark chuckled, warming quickly to his new neighbor. "Come on in. I'm still getting things sorted out, so don't mind the mess."

Leo's gaze swept the room and he couldn't hide his disgust. "I see you're going for a retro look. I'm not sure it's working. The couch really sucks. I won't bother commenting on the chairs. But the word hideous comes to mind."

"This stuff is rented. I'm not usually in town long enough to worry about furnishings. I live mostly in hotels when I'm on assignment."

"So Francie said. The couch would look much better facing the fireplace. And perhaps you could flank the wing chairs on either side of it." Leo tapped his chin with his forefinger, mentally rearranging the room. "You're not going to be able to hide the ugly things, so you may as well make them the focal point of the room. Sort of an in-your-face statement."

Seeing the wisdom of the suggestion, Mark nodded. "Thanks. Are you a decorator, by any chance?"

"Not all gay men are decorators—that's just a vicious rumor being circulated by followers of Jerry Falwell." The blond man grinned mischievously. "Some of us are hairdressers. But I do dabble in both, from time to time.

"Actually, I don't have a full-time job. I live off a trust fund, which allows me to indulge my hobbies, one of which is interior design. And I do haircuts free of charge. If you're game, drop by sometime. But not too early. I'm a late sleeper."

Mark plowed fingers through his hair, knowing he needed a trim. "Thanks. I'll keep that in mind. Care for a glass of wine?" He liked Leo. The man was refreshingly honest, very charming and utterly outrageous.

Leo nodded. "Wine is my passion. Another hobby, I'm afraid, and a very expensive one. I'm into vintage wines. I collect them. Mostly California cabs and merlots. I'm a bit of a snob. Don't care much for the French bordeaux. Highly overrated, in my opinion. Their soil's depleted from years of doing business as usual. They need to get into the twenty-first century and quit resting on their laurels. Food? Yes, definitely. They can rest all they want. But wine? I think not."

Mark's brow shot up at the man's unorthodox

opinion. He didn't know much about wine, but he'd always heard that French wines were the best.

Opening the gift bottle of Joseph Phelps' Insignia, he handed Leo a glass of the deep red wine, then offered him a seat on the ugly sofa. "I guess Francie told you about my job with the Associated Press?"

"She did. I must say I'm impressed. I've always been a nut about photography, though I can't take a decent photo to save my life. They're either overexposed, underexposed or totally out of focus. Maybe I need glasses."

"Perhaps I can give you some hints, to thank you for the wine. It's simple, once you get the hang of it."

"I'd appreciate that. I've been thinking about buying one of those digital cameras." He sipped his wine, sighed with pleasure, and then asked, "How do you like Francie? She's a very special woman, our Francie, though a bit flighty when it comes to men. She hasn't met the right one yet, I suspect. Though I can tell you that if I were straight she'd be one female I'd lob on to. A more loyal woman you could never ask for. And she's a real sweetheart, too."

Arching his right brow, Mark tried to keep the incredulity out of his voice. "Really? I don't know her that well. Does she have a boyfriend?"

"I knew it." Leo appeared pleased with himself and Mark's question. "You two would be perfect for each other. And no, she doesn't. Francie narrowly escaped getting married recently. The guy was gorgeous and a real sweetie, but she wasn't in love with him. No spark, if you get my drift."

"That must have been a difficult decision for her to make."

"Francie's got a phobia when it comes to marriage. I think it's because her mother wants it so badly. Josephine Morelli is a breed unto herself. You'll meet her, if you stay here long enough. She's got a nose for single men. You're single, right?"

"Very much so."

"Thought so. I can usually spot them. But don't worry. I only hit on the ones I know share my lifestyle. So, how do you feel about marriage?"

"It's a great institution, though I'm not ready to give up my career just yet and settle down. The woman who could make me do that would have to be very special. I'm pretty much married to my job."

Leo's eyes twinkled. "Very special, indeed," he said, gulping down the rest of his wine. "Well, guess I'd better go. I have a date with the lovely Francesca tonight. We're going out to celebrate my birthday— the big three-oh. Care to join us? My treat."

"Uh, thanks for the offer, but I've got some work to do, not to mention unpacking, so I'd better take a rain check." When he wooed Francie, he wanted to do it alone, out of sight of Leo, who seemed too astute for his own good. The man didn't miss much, that was for sure.

"Well, if you change your mind, we'll be at Le Bec Fin. Dinner's at seven. Ask any cabbie how to get there. If you can't make dinner, try for dessert. I've ordered a special soufflé.

"Francie is the only woman I know who shares my passion for food and sweets. All the others worry about their weight. We've sort of become dining buddies."

"Have a great time. And happy birthday!"

Once Leo departed, Mark took the time to mull over their conversation, especially as it pertained to Josephine Morelli. If he got Francie's mother to be his ally, it could hasten the wooing process. He wanted revenge, but he didn't want to spend the rest of his life getting it.

From what Leo had said, Mrs. Morelli was looking for a prospective son-in-law. Mark was looking to drag Francie to the altar. It sounded like a match made in heaven.

"SORRY I'M LATE, Leo. Things kept popping up at work, and Ted's useless when it comes to finding paperwork that he's misplaced. I swear, the man couldn't find his butt if it wasn't attached. And then I couldn't find a cab to save my life. I must look a mess." Francie patted her hair, which was curling every which way. She hated her curls, considering them to be an unruly mess.

Leo smiled, squeezing her hand in a calming fashion then filled her wineglass. "I'm used to my own company, sweetie, so your being a tad late doesn't bother me in the least. Besides, I entertained myself this afternoon by paying a visit to our new resident hunk. Brought him a bottle of wine as a welcome gift. I must say the man is primo."

Unbuttoning her coat, Francie dropped into her seat and stared at Leo in wide-eyed disbelief. "Do you mean Mark Fielding?" Of course he meant Mark.

Who else would he mean? There were no other new tenants in the building, certainly none that could be classified as hunks.

"He's charming, your Mr. Fielding. I think you two would make the perfect couple, and I'll be seriously displeased if you don't hook up with him."

Her cheeks filled with color. "He's not *my* Mr. Fielding. Have you been watching *Pride and Prejudice* again? You sound very Jane Austen this evening." She shook her head. Leo was infatuated with Colin Firth, not that she could blame him. The actor who portrayed Mr. Darcy in the A&E production was adorable.

"My God! I hope you didn't say anything to Mark along those lines. I'd be mortified to speak to him again, if you did." And she had no intention of getting involved with the man, despite the fact that he made her toes tingle.

"Well, of course not," Leo lied, swallowing his smile. "Give me more credit than that, sweetie. I just asked him what he thought of you and he replied that he really didn't know you very well. Then he offered to teach me how to use a camera properly. Isn't that nice?"

Francie released the breath she'd been holding. She was determined not to get involved with any man for a very long time, eons possibly, and especially not someone who was a potential client, and certainly not someone with whom Leo had brokered a match.

The man was worse than a woman when it came to matchmaking. Leo was notorious for choosing horrible dates. He had once set her up with a florist whom he'd sworn was perfect for her. The man had turned out to be married with six children. Then there was the plastic surgeon who insisted he could give Francie bigger and better boobs at a discount.

Okay, so she wasn't Pamela Anderson, but she wasn't flat, either. And hers were real!

Francie decided a long time ago that she could screw up her life on her own. She didn't need Leo to aid her.

"I hope you don't mind, but I suggested to Mark that he join us for dessert. He said he couldn't make dinner."

"What?" Francie's mouth fell open, then she snapped it shut. "You invited him to join us? Whatever for?"

"Because he's a nice guy, it's my birthday and I can do whatever I want. I am paying, after all."

She had the grace to blush. "I did offer, Leo."

"I know, sweetie, but I've got gobs more money than you, and no one to spend it on but myself, so it seemed silly to have you pay."

Leo was very generous with his money. Francie wouldn't dine out nearly as much as she did, if that weren't the case. Of course, she'd probably be ten pounds thinner.

"What did you buy me? I've been conjuring up all sorts of delicious possibilities." Leo tried peering into her purse, so Francie picked it up and moved it to the other side of the table. "Too small for a Porsche. Pity," he said, grinning.

Leo was like a child when it came to receiving gifts. In the three years they'd lived together, Francie had learned that he not only liked surprises, he wanted a big fuss made over his birthday, and pretty much every other holiday on the calendar, be it Jewish or secular.

He said it was because he'd been raised by his aunt and uncle after his parents died—a couple of religious fanatics who didn't know how to have fun, didn't celebrate Christmas or any other "heathen" holiday, and certainly hadn't approved when Leo came out of the closet at age eighteen to announce that he was leaving home to live with another man...in sin.

That had been the last time he'd heard from his relatives. Fortunately the trust fund from his parents had kicked in shortly after that; he'd been supporting himself ever since. And pretty much spitting in the eye of anyone who didn't like his lifestyle, or him.

Francie not only adored Leo, she admired him greatly.

Reaching into her purse, she extracted a small box and laid it on the plate in front of him. The gift had set her back quite a bit, but she figured her friend was worth it. "I hope you like it. I spent hours looking for just the right one."

Tearing open the blue foil wrapping paper, Leo's eyes brightened with anticipation. "I can't imagine what it is," he said, lifting the lid on the black velvet box to find a gold money clip engraved with his initials. "I love it! I've always wanted a money clip. How did you know?"

Francie's smile was filled with indulgence. "Your hints are not altogether subtle, Leo, but they are effective. Happy birthday!" Leaning toward him, she kissed his cheek.

Le Bec Fin was one of Philadelphia's finest restaurants, and Leo and Francie gorged themselves on two dozen oysters, rare beef Wellington and the most scrumptious chocolate soufflé ever whipped up by a mere mortal.

Leaning back in her chair, Francie sighed, wondering if her skirt would still fit in the morning. She rather doubted it. "That was delicious. I'm totally stuffed." And totally relieved that Mark hadn't put in an appearance tonight. She wasn't sure she could handle him after sharing two bottles of wine with Leo. Or should she say—she wasn't sure she could handle herself?

LEO AND FRANCIE had just entered their apartment when Francie ground to a halt. Leo, following close on her heels, colliding with her back. In her inebriated condition, it was a wonder she didn't fall over on her face.

"Damn! I left my briefcase in your car. I've got to run down and get it. There are papers in it that I need to go over before I leave for work tomorrow. Ted will kill me if I'm not prepared for our meeting."

"Just leave it. You can get it in the morning."

She mulled over his suggestion, then shook her head, which was a huge mistake. It was pounding. She rubbed her temples to ease the throbbing, but to no avail. "Give me your keys. I won't be a minute."

"If you insist." He dangled them from his fingertips, kissed her cheek, and told her good-night. "Be careful," he shouted over his shoulder. "This might be a good neighborhood, but it's still filled with perverts. I'm living proof of that."

"Wonderful. Maybe I'll get lucky and meet one." She shut the door behind her and hurried to the elevator. They lived on the tenth floor, so it took a few minutes for the ancient conveyance to reach the lobby.

After retrieving her briefcase—an uneventful trip...not a pervert in sight—she dashed back into the historic stone building, rubbing her arms briskly against the cold wind, and waited impatiently for the elevator to descend.

Her head was splitting in two and she wanted nothing more than to take a hot bath, pop a few aspirin, and climb into bed.

The door to the elevator finally opened and she stepped in. Believing she was alone, Francie nearly jumped out of her skin when she discovered she wasn't.

"Hello again. Did you have a good time tonight?"

Swiveling, she looked up into the handsome face of Mark Fielding. Normally, Francie would care that she looked like shit. But since she felt the same way, she wasn't overly concerned that her hair was sticking out in twelve different directions, like Medusa on speed, and that her eyeliner had smeared, giving her that *Adams Family* look. She hadn't a smidgen of lipstick on, and her stomach was bloated and sticking out as if she were six months' pregnant.

She was a scary sight at best.

Francie managed a smile, though it came out looking more like a grimace. "Leo and I had a great time. Perhaps too good a time. My head feels like an anvil fell on it. And I'm old enough to know better."

"I bet you've got tension in your neck."

She was about to agree—her neck felt like a huge knotted oak—when he reached out and began to massage the muscles there. His hands were warm, and so was she getting to be. "I'm very good at this," he said, making her wonder what else he was good at.

Sighing at the delicious way he was making her feel, she agreed. "Yes...yes, you are. But I'm sure an aspirin will take care of my headache." She tried to pull back, but he had a firm grip and didn't release her.

"It's not the same as having your neck rubbed. Trust me. I know what I'm talking about. Guess Leo had wine with dinner, huh?"

She groaned in ecstasy as his thumbs made circles at the base of her neck, hardly able to believe it was her own voice she was hearing. And then she came to her senses. "Um, thank you very much, Mark. The massage helped a great deal."

Of course, now she had tension much lower than her neck. Like below her waist.

Damn!

Francie was relieved when the elevator stopped and opened. "Well, here we are," she announced, rather stupidly.

"I'll walk you to your door."

"That's not necessary! It's just down the hall."

"I wouldn't be much of a gentleman if I didn't, now would I?"

Sighing, Francie nodded in defeat, wondering when her twenty-first-century sensibilities were going to kick in and she would burst into a chorus of "I Am Woman." Though instead of roaring, she was purring like a damned cat in heat.

At her door, they stopped, and Mark gazed down into her eyes. His eyes were filled with something that looked suspiciously like passion. Francie felt her knees quiver.

Or was that something else?

"You look very nice tonight."

"I'm a mess, but thanks." Her new red-silk Liz Claiborne suit was horribly wrinkled, not to mention stained, thanks to her enthusiasm for crème frêche.

"A woman who looks disheveled, like she's just gotten out of bed, is very enticing."

Her mouth went dry. "Well, that's exactly where I'm headed, so I'll say good-night and thanks again."

Practically slamming the door in Mark's face, Francie leaned heavily against it. She could hear his amused chuckle recede as he headed down the hall to his own apartment.

"Damn cocky male!"

Damn stupid woman!

5

TED BAXTER FANCIED himself as somewhat of a ladies' man, which was ludicrous considering Francie's boss was about the same size as Danny DeVito but lacked the actor's sparkling personality, sense of humor or talent.

The president of Ted Baxter Promotions was arrogant, self-serving and dull, which probably accounted for the fact that he'd been divorced three times and was still looking for the perfect trophy wife to take the edge off his dullness. He was also a terrible businessman.

Francie got along fine with her boss, having made it clear two years ago when she accepted the job as his assistant that she wasn't interested in trying out any "other" positions that he might have in mind. And she was pretty sure he'd had several.

Ted relied on her, and she relied on the biweekly paycheck she received in return. It wasn't a perfect arrangement, but it was "doable," as Ted was fond of saying.

"We've got a problem, Francesca." Ted always called her by her given name, believing Francie was too cutesy for the public relations business. "I've got the IRS breathing down my neck. Things have reached a crisis stage."

Surprise! Surprise!

No doubt Ted hadn't sent in his quarterly payments again, preferring instead to take the money owed to the government and lavish gifts on his latest girlfriend, whom he claimed was an actress, but whom Francie was fairly certain was a high-priced call girl.

I mean, really! Hardly anyone was named Peaches these days!

"The quarterly reports?" she asked.

He shook his head, looking defeated and suddenly old for his fifty-eight years, despite the fact that he'd dyed his hair black and had a tummy tuck. "Nothing so simple, I'm afraid. I'm behind on my income taxes," he said, surprising her.

She'd come to the meeting this morning prepared to discuss the Langley Real Estate account—no easy feat, considering how hungover she was from Leo's birthday party—but that was obviously not what this meeting was about.

"The penalties are killing me," he went on. "I've got to bring in more revenue or we're going to be put out of business."

Shifting in her seat, Francie wondered why Ted was confiding personal financial details to her. That wasn't usually his style. Ted much preferred glossing over matters, making everything seem perfect and rosy. The man was a master at B.S. "Is there anything I can do to help? Perhaps call the IRS and try to make arrangements to—"

"Don't you think I've already done that? Hell, my accountant's becoming personal friends with the IRS agent in charge of my case. Damn blood-sucking bastard. The whole lot of them are bastards. Why can't they leave honest businessmen alone?"

Honest being the operative word, Francie thought.

Business had been slow of late, which was why she had tried so desperately to entice Mark Fielding to sign with the company. So far he hadn't committed. "I have Mr. Fielding close to signing," she said, crossing her fingers behind her back and hoping her optimism would pay off.

Ted stopped pacing and halted in front of her chair. "How close? We need his business, not to mention the hefty deposit he'll give us to proceed with his publicity campaign."

"I'm...I'm not sure. He's checking out a few more firms, trying to make the best choice possible. I was planning to call him next week to see if he's made a decision."

"We need Fielding, Francesca. Call him today. Do *whatever*—" he emphasized the word in his smarmy way "—you have to do to sign him. Wine and dine him, become his best friend, let him know you're *interested*...in a purely professional capacity, of course."

Of course, my ass!

"I'm up to my ears in debt, and if you want to keep your job, then you've got to help me."

Francie tried hard to maintain her composure. Ted had screwed everything up and now it was suddenly her responsibility to fix it? That was rich. And totally unfair.

"One account isn't going to do that much good, is it?" And she certainly didn't intend to sell herself to save Baxter Promotions. She did want to save her job, however—a job she loved and was getting darn good at.

"I've got several things in the works, including some associates who may be willing to invest in the company for the short term. But they need to be convinced that we are attracting clients, and that those clients are completely satisfied with our services. No one wants to kiss a pig."

Yeah? What about your girlfriend, Ted?

"I took a chance when I hired you, Francesca, because you were young and inexperienced. But I liked your aggressiveness, your willingness to try. I hope my faith in you hasn't been misplaced."

"I'll do my best." Francie knew the reason Ted had hired her. She'd been willing to work cheap just to get her foot in the door. Now that foot was getting stomped on.

"Do better than that, Francesca. Your job and my business depend on your signing Fielding, understand?"

Francie nodded, hating Ted Baxter at that moment. Perhaps she should look for another job. But she was so tired of not sticking things out. It was bad enough that her love life was a total disaster due to her penchant for quitting midstream. She didn't want that to become her M.O. in her professional life, as well.

"I'll sign Fielding. Don't worry."

He smiled widely. She was pretty sure he'd had caps put on his teeth; they were a little too perfect and not tobacco stained, as they once were. "That's what I like to hear. Now get on it at once. See if he wants to have dinner tonight. You can expense it, just don't order soup to nuts, okay?"

"I understand perfectly what's expected of me."

She just wasn't certain Mark Fielding would.

"I'M YOUR BEST FRIEND, Francie, so I'm just going to come right out and say what I have to say. I don't want you to be upset, okay? Try to remember that we've been friends since first grade and I love you like a sister."

As if this morning's meeting with Ted hadn't been painful enough, now Joyce is going to dump on me, Francie thought.

"Like I could stop you." Francie smiled at the absurdity of the idea. No one muzzled Joyce Rialto and lived to talk about it. The redhead was a walking, talking opinion, who didn't mince words when she thought she was right about something, which was most of the time. And since Francie had a pretty good idea of what her friend was about to say, she couldn't really blame her.

"This probably isn't a good time to remind you that you hate your sister."

Joyce ignored the teasing comment. "I'm sorry, Francie, but I can't afford to be in any more of your weddings. I work at Neiman's, not Fort Knox. These weddings of yours are costing me a small fortune in ugly bridesmaid dresses, even with my ten percent employee discount. It's not like I can ever wear them again.

"As much as I want to stand up for you, be with you on your special day, I just can't do it again. You'll have to find someone else."

Setting down her bowl of ice cream, Francie clicked off the video they'd been watching and reached out to take her friend's hand. "Joyce, I'm sorry. I never meant to create problems for you. Maybe someday I'll be able to reimburse you for—"

The redhead shook her head. "I don't want your money. I just want you to stop placating your mother. These relationships you keep entering into have been destructive…to everyone concerned, not just you. I've hesitated saying anything up till now, but three weddings are just too much. This has got to stop."

"I know that. Don't you think I know that? And I've already told my mom that I'm not making the walk down the aisle again, no matter how much she begs. I'm through with bridal shows, caterers and weddings, but mostly I'm through with men."

Eyes widening in surprise, Joyce said, "No need to get drastic, Francie. Men serve their purpose." Her mood changed instantly and she grew animated. "Eddie's taking me to New York City next week to see *Mama Mia*. I can't wait. I bought the soundtrack and memorized the lyrics to all the songs."

"Hey, I thought we were going to see that musical together. You know how much I like Abba." They'd been planning the trip for months. Just the two of them, like when they were younger and used to take the train to New York City and pretend they were appearing on Broadway.

With an apologetic sigh, Joyce replied, "After your

last wedding I couldn't afford the ticket, Francie. When Eddie offered, I jumped at the chance. Besides, we might stay at the Plaza. It was a hard invitation to resist."

"But you don't even like Eddie Bertucci that much. You said he had sweat gland problems." Translation: Eddie smelled.

"So what? I don't have to marry him. That's something you need to learn. You can go out, have sex, dinner, whatever, and you don't have to get engaged. It's a new concept called dating. You should try it sometime."

"Very funny." Francie heaved a sigh. "I'm so disappointed, Joyce. I was really looking forward to going with you. It's been ages since we've been to New York City together."

"Maybe Leo will take you. He loves musicals. Why don't you ask him?"

"Leo's seen the play four times already. I don't think he's up for a fifth. Besides, Leo pays for everything. If I invited him to go, he'd feel obligated to pay for the tickets. He's too generous for his own good."

The apartment they shared was proof of that. Leo had paid for most of the furnishings, except for her bedroom suite, which Francie had brought from home and Leo hated. The maple pieces didn't meet his artistic sensibilities, he'd said.

Leo had hired painters and wallpaper hangers, had drapes and shutters custom made. The dwelling was decorated in what Joyce called "Lord of the Manor" or English country. Heavy furniture, rich fabrics, lovely accessories, all tastefully put together and paid for by Leo.

Francie felt a little bit like Cinderella every time she entered the charming apartment. It overlooked Rittenhouse Square and positively oozed with antiquity and character.

"I could use a man like that. Too bad Leo's gay. Maybe I should try and convert him." Joyce laughed at her own joke, then said, "So how did your mother take the news? Did her head spin around? Did she foam at the mouth, then spew green stuff all over the carpet?"

"No, nothing like that. Josephine just ignored everything I said, like she usually does. But I won't be wheedled, cajoled or made to feel guilty this time. I've made up my mind to remain single."

"Permanently?" Joyce frowned. "Don't you ever want to get married and have kids? I thought we talked about buying houses next door to each other and raising our kids together. How can we do that if you don't get married?"

"We were twelve at the time, Joyce. Things have changed. I've changed. I'm just not interested in all that domestic stuff now. I'm focused on my career—" such as it was "—on enjoying myself, meeting new and interesting people."

"Ah, so there's a new man in your life, is that it?"

At Joyce's astuteness, Francie felt heat rise up her neck—the very neck so recently massaged by— "Not exactly. We have a new tenant in the building, and he also happens to be a potential client of our firm."

Picking up her bowl of nearly melted chocolate ice

cream, Joyce began eating. "I knew it. You've got that 'Here Comes the Bride' look on your face again."

"Don't be ridiculous! I hardly know Mark. We've only just met." And she certainly wasn't looking for a groom.

Now the wedding night on the other hand...

"Convenient that he lives in the same building as you."

"That's not a crime, merely a coincidence."

"Since I don't believe in coincidences, I guess I'll just chalk it up to fate. So what's this Mark do for a living? Why does he need a publicist?"

Preferring strawberry to chocolate, Francie licked her spoon, savoring the cold taste on her tongue, before answering. "He's a photojournalist for the Associated Press. His first book is going to be published next year, and he might want Baxter Promotions to help him with the publicity campaign."

"Is he cute?"

Francie considered the question a moment. "Not cute, as in Brad Pitt cute, but he's very handsome, as in Pierce Brosnan handsome."

And she was totally enamored of him, despite her best intentions not to be. Dammit!

"Ohmigod! I can't believe you are opening yourself up to another relationship with yet another heart-throb. Matt Carson was adorable, as I recall. And a very nice man."

"It's not like that. I'm not interested in Mark in a romantic sense."

Did sex count as romance?

Stop it, Francie! You cannot have sex with Mark Fielding.

Of course, a kiss or two wouldn't be out of the—

"Well, maybe you should be. Maybe you should just have a good, old-fashioned bout of mind-blowing sex and get it out of your system." As soon as the words were out of her mouth, Joyce slapped her forehead. "What the hell am I saying? You try to marry everyone you have sex with. Never mind. Forget I said that. Just tell Ted to work with this guy, if he signs on. Keep your distance. You'll be much happier in the long run if you do."

She had no intention of confiding to Joyce what Ted Baxter had in mind for Mark Fielding, so she stretched the truth a bit. "I'm sure that's exactly what will happen. Ted always takes the good clients for himself. I usually end up with the ones he doesn't want."

"Good. Now turn the movie back on. If I'm not going to have sex tonight, I may as well watch someone else doing it. I know I wouldn't be able to stay faithful with that sexy French guy in my bed."

They'd been watching *Unfaithful* with Richard Gere, Diane Lane and some hunky French actor. "If you were married to Richard Gere, you might feel differently about that. I know I would."

"True. But since I'm not I'll just lust quietly over here and live vicariously through our adulterous heroine. Any man who could pick me up and toss me over his shoulder would be worth making love to."

At five-foot-nine, one hundred and fifty-five pounds, Joyce was a big girl who only dated men six feet and over. She didn't have many criteria when it came to men—usually they just had to be breathing—but she did like them to be taller than she was and to outweigh her by at least twenty pounds.

Mark Fielding was well over six feet, probably by two inches. He could pick Joyce up with one hand, though Francie wasn't about to tell her best friend that.

The mere fact that she knew how tall Mark was would send Joyce into another lecture and, quite frankly, Francie was getting sick and tired of all the lectures, from everyone.

No. Francie would do her job, which was to sign Mark Fielding on the dotted line. Theirs would be strictly a working relationship. She had no intention of getting involved with Mark—romantically or any other way.

She was a professional businesswoman with a good head on her shoulders. Despite her reputation for being flighty, she was smart, sexy—*okay, sort of sexy!*—and best of all—single. And she intended to stay that way.

6

JOSEPHINE MORELLI was not happy with her ungrateful, misguided daughter. In fact, she was very disturbed.

Francie had strange ideas in her head about marriage and children, and it was a mother's job to fix that, to set her daughter straight. No self-respecting woman would choose a career over having babies! It was unthinkable.

In Josephine's mind, there was only one solution to the current problem. Francie had fallen off the proverbial horse. She needed to get back on and to face the fear of riding, er, matrimony head-on. The way to do that was to find Francie a new fiancé, and quickly. As her mother, she was duty bound to accomplish that feat.

Once the red light had changed to green, Josephine hurried across the busy intersection, ignoring the honking horns and traffic congestion. She passed historic Rittenhouse Square and headed toward her daughter's apartment building, ruminating about the first three prospective bridegrooms and how she had made such unfortunate mistakes.

The first man she had chosen had been too full of himself, too loud and brash, not refined enough for her cosmopolitan daughter, not to mention that he looked like Bill Clinton. She was sorry to lose the discount on the burial plots—she and John weren't getting any younger—but that was out of her hands now.

The second one had been too meek and mild for Francie. A nice man, but a Casper Milquetoast nonetheless. Josephine could see that now.

Matt Carson had been a very nice boy, and that most likely had been the problem. He'd been too young and immature, too willing to let Francie have her way about everything.

Francie needed someone strong. She needed a take-charge man who would set down the law—an old-fashioned husband who wanted a wife, in the truest sense of the word.

Love, honor and obey.

Have children!

Entering the twelve-story building, Josephine waved to the white-haired, stoop-shouldered doorman and wondered how Lester Phipps would be able to carry anyone's groceries let alone apprehend an intruder if it became necessary. She shook her head, knowing such things were impossible.

Esther Phipps was an acquaintance of hers and had confided that her husband was on Viagra. Josephine had concluded that the only thing Lester could lift—and not very often, according to Esther—was his dick.

Josephine and John still had a very active sex life. Her husband needed no pills to make him virile. He was Italian, after all! But these things she kept to herself. The younger generation talked too much about matters better left in the privacy of the bedroom.

Lisa was the worst offender, always telling the most intimate details about the men she dated, and how on a few occasions she'd used one of those vibrating machines. John had nearly passed out when he'd heard that!

Hurrying to catch the elevator, Josephine swallowed her fear. She wasn't afraid of much, but hated confined spaces, and the elevator looked older than she was. But she was in no shape to walk up ten flights of stairs.

The last wedding fiasco had done serious damage to her health. How she was still living was a mystery. Dr. Mancini had said she was fine, just overwrought because of her disappointment at Francie's behavior. But what did that old fool know about anything? A woman knew when her days were numbered. Death was imminent. She was sure of it. She only hoped that her family would give her a nice send-off when the time came.

The gold doors were just starting to close when a tall man rushed forward, shouting for her to hold the elevator. Josephine complied, hoping he wasn't a masher. It would be just her luck to get stuck in an elevator with a rapist. A woman couldn't be too careful these days, and she was still attractive for her age. Everyone said so.

The man was strongly built and had very nice blue eyes. Josephine could judge a man's character by his eyes, and she thought this one was a good egg.

"Thanks for holding the door, ma'am."

Nice manners, too!

"You're welcome. I'm going to the tenth floor. What button do you want me to push for you?"

"I'm on ten, too."

Josephine's brow arched. "I don't live in this building. I'm on my way up to see my daughter. Sometimes on the weekends I like to surprise her."

"Are you Francesca Morelli's mother, by any chance?"

Narrowing her eyes suspiciously, she studied the stranger. "How do you know that? You're not with the government, are you?"

He swallowed his smile. "No, ma'am. The family resemblance is remarkable."

She nodded. "Yes, Francie looks like me. My other daughter, Lisa, looks like John, my husband. Don't tell Lisa I said so, but I think Francie made out better. The Abrizzi women have good genes. My mother has skin like a seventy-year-old."

"Really? How interesting."

"How well do you know my daughter?"

"Not well. I just moved in a few days ago." He held out his hand. "Mark Fielding. Nice to meet you. Your daughter and I have a professional working relationship, of sorts. I'm considering signing with her company."

"You're an actor?" Josephine couldn't hide her disgust or disappointment. Actors were a shiftless, lazy lot. Lisa had dated one last year, and he was always reciting lines from Shakespeare. The man was no Robert De Niro, that was for sure.

Mark shook his head and she noticed what a nice,

full head of dark hair he had and wondered if he was Italian, perhaps on his mother's side. "I'm a photographer for the Associated Press."

Josephine's eyes lit with admiration. "I bet you make a very good living at that." Enough to support a wife and family, she was certain.

"I do. I'm single, so it doesn't take that much to live on. I'm able to save a considerable amount of money every month."

A man with a savings account was a find. A handsome unmarried man with a savings account was not to be passed up. And if he was Italian...

"So you're single? What a shame. A nice-looking man like you?" She paused a moment. "Are you one of those gay men? Is that why you're not married?" Unfortunately these matters had to be considered in this day and age.

His grin was engaging and Josephine was suitably impressed. The man was sexier than De Niro. "Nope. I just never found the right woman. I'm eager to find a wife and settle down."

Josephine's hand went to her racing heart. "That's wonderful! So many young people don't appreciate the sanctity of marriage and family."

"Well, I'm not one of them. I realize how important it is to form a lasting relationship with someone you love. And I absolutely adore children. I'd like to have a large family someday, maybe five or six kids."

Making the sign of the cross, Josephine said a silent prayer of thanks.

"Do you have any grandchildren, Mrs. Morelli?"

The hated question haunted her. "No." She shook

her head and pursed her lips. "My daughters have not done their duty. I'm upset that I don't have *bambinos* to dote on. A woman should have grandchildren to brighten her days."

The elevator shook to a halt and the doors opened. Mark allowed Josephine to precede him out. They walked down the hall together in companionable silence, Josephine going over wedding plans once again, Mark congratulating himself on such good fortune at having run into Francie's mother.

When they turned the corner, they spotted Francie standing in front of Mark's door.

"Ah, there's my daughter now. Isn't she beautiful? Such a woman, and smart, too. A mother's pride and joy. If only Francie were married with children, she'd be perfect."

Josephine started waving. "Yoo-hoo! Francie! It's your mother. I just met the nicest man in the elevator. He says he knows you."

AT THE SOUND of her mother's voice, Francie turned and groaned inwardly. Leave it to Josephine to find another eligible bachelor to fix her up with. And Mark Fielding, no less.

Does my luck stink or what?

She'd come to Mark's apartment to invite him to dinner and to press him about his promotion plans. Now she not only had that challenge ahead of her, she had to deal with her mother, too.

Pasting on a smile, she replied, "Ma, what a nice surprise! Hello, Mark. I was just coming by to see you."

Apparently pleased by that news, Mark smiled. "I've just met your mother. We've had a lovely chat."

Francie could just imagine what the two of them had talked about: grandchildren—or Josephine's lack of them. That was her mother's favorite topic of conversation, in addition to her supposedly failing health.

"I will wait for you in your apartment, Francesca. I'm tired and need to put my feet up."

Failing to notice the triumphant gleam in her mother's eyes, Francie breathed a sigh of relief, grateful Josephine wasn't going to try to play matchmaker again. "Okay, Ma. I'll be there in a minute."

"Was there something you needed, Francie?" Mark asked, inserting the key in the lock and opening the door to his apartment. "Come on in. Just don't remark on my furniture. Leo has already given me an earful about it."

Francie grinned. "Leo's only one of my opinionated friends. I'm afraid I'm surrounded by them."

"Leo's great. He gave me a few decorating tips, told me how to rearrange the furniture. I didn't mind the help. I'm not good at that sort of thing."

What the apartment lacked in decorating flair, it made up for in neatness. "It looks like you've unpacked."

"I didn't have that much to work with, so it didn't take long. I'm glad you stopped over today."

Francie felt heat rise to her cheeks. "I came to invite you to dinner this evening. I thought perhaps we could discuss plans for your publicity campaign. If you're ready to proceed, that is."

"That'd be great. What time shall I come by your apartment to get you?"

"Um, it might be easier if I come by and get you. Leo's staying in tonight, and if he starts asking questions about photography, we're likely to be held up for hours."

"Fine with me. What kind of wine do you like, red or white?"

Francie smiled. "When you live with someone like Leo, there is only one type of wine. Tell you what, I'll raid his wine cabinet and bring a bottle over."

"Sounds good. What time shall I expect you?"

Francie glanced down at her watch. It was already three o'clock. It would take her an hour to get rid of her mother, another hour to bathe and do her nails. Then there was trying to decide what to wear, not to mention she had to make dinner reservations somewhere. "I'll come by around seven."

Mark walked her to the door. "I'm looking forward to tonight, Francie. Thanks for asking me to dinner. If you hadn't, I was going to ask you."

She felt heat rise up her cheeks. "Oh, well. It's just business, and so I thought—"

Mark's phone rang. "Gotta run. Catch you later, okay?"

Francie hoped Mark didn't get the wrong idea about her dinner invitation. She didn't want to mislead him into thinking that what she had planned was more than dinner—in spite of Ted's not-so-subtle hints that she throw herself at the man.

Bedding Mark was certainly not a distasteful idea, just a bad one!

A few moments later she entered her apartment to find her mother asleep on the sofa and Leo nowhere in sight. Or perhaps Josephine had just been lying in wait, ready to pounce, because she awoke immediately—a little too quickly, Francie thought—when Francie entered the living room.

"So tell me everything, Francesca. Why were you waiting for Mark Fielding? He's such a nice man. You could do worse. In fact, you have done worse."

"Please, Ma, don't start. It's a business meeting, nothing more. I need Mark to sign a contract with Baxter Promotions, so I invited him to dinner to encourage him to do just that. I have no intention of entering into another relationship with a man."

"What are you going to wear to this dinner? You should wear something sexy, maybe black, and show some bosom. A little cleavage couldn't hurt."

Shaking her head, Francie finally smiled and plopped down next to her mother on the sofa. "You are a very bad lady, Ma. I hope you know that. Cleavage, indeed!"

"Why? Because I want my daughter to impress a nice gentleman?"

"You're my mother. You should be telling me to cover up and wear high-necked dresses, not expose myself. What kind of a mother tells her daughter that?"

"A desperate one. Men like women who are sexy. I'm trying to help you find a man. I admit I made mistakes with the last three."

Francie's eyes widened. Her mother never admitted to being wrong. "You do?"

Josephine nodded. "I thought it over on the way here, and I realized that I had chosen poorly for you. Those men weren't strong enough. You need to be taken in hand, by someone who can lay down the law."

Francie began laughing hysterically.

"What? What did I say? Why are you laughing like a crazy woman?"

"Because you drive me nuts, that's why. I'm not getting married. I told you that. Why do you refuse to listen when I tell you how I feel?"

"You've had a run of bad luck. You haven't met the right man yet. Or if you have, you don't realize it. It was my fault for pushing you in the wrong direction. I think I've found the right one this time."

Francie's mouth fell open. "I hope you're not talking about Mark Fielding. He's a potential client, not a suitor. And you'd better forget all about playing matchmaker, Ma, because if you don't, I'm never going to forgive you."

"I don't need to play matchmaker this time. I'm just going to let nature take its course and see what happens."

"Where do you come up with this stuff? Have you been watching *Dr. Phil* again?"

"That man is a saint. But no, I only know from experience as a woman and a mother that you and Mr. Fielding have an attraction between you. I've seen it with my own eyes."

"You only see what you want to see, Ma. There's nothing going on between us."

"The man looks at you like he's hungry. Your father used to look at me like that, so I know what I'm talking about. A man knows what he wants, and he goes out and gets it."

"Well, that's just peachy for Mr. Fielding, but I am not interested in him, for any reason other than to bring him into our company. He's a nice guy, but Mark is not my type."

Liar! Liar! Liar!

Oh, shut up!

"What is he, blood? Type, schmype. I know nothing about type, only about spark. And you two have plenty of that."

"This discussion is over. I'm not going to tell you again, okay?"

Josephine rose to her feet. "When I'm dead and buried you'll be sorry that you spoke to me this way, Francesca. I'm your mother. You should show respect."

"And I'm your daughter. Your grown daughter, I might add. Don't I deserve the same consideration?"

"Come to dinner tomorrow. Promise me, Francesca, or I won't be able to sleep a wink tonight. I can feel the acid churning in my stomach. Soon it'll be at my throat, and then I will die of cancer. It can kill you, that acid. And—"

Francie heaved a sigh. "Okay, okay, I'll be there. Is Aunt Flo coming, too?"

"Of course, she's coming. Florence is my sister. I had to invite her. She's all alone, just like you'll be if you don't wise up and listen to your mother."

Allowing her mother to have the last word, Francie urged her toward the door, handed the woman her coat and kissed her goodbye. "I'll see you tomorrow, Ma. Give Dad a kiss for me, okay?" Then she shut the door and leaned against it, praying that tomorrow would never come.

And wondering how she was going to get through tonight, now that her mother had put all sorts of fanciful, ridiculous, not-to-be-believed-under-no-uncertain-terms romantic notions in her head.

She wished just this once she was Jewish because there was only one way to describe her feelings at the moment. *Oy Vey!*

7

"I'M GLAD you suggested we walk home tonight, Francie. It's a perfect evening. And it'll give us a chance to burn up a few more calories, not that you need to lose weight." Francie had a fantastic body—one that Mark intended to explore more thoroughly, and very soon.

He'd been surprised by her dinner invitation this afternoon. And though Mark knew it was to entice him to sign on the dotted line, he intended to turn it to his advantage. "Thanks again for inviting me out. Dinner was great."

"When are you going to put me out of my misery, Mark, and tell me what you've decided about signing with Baxter Promotions? You've evaded the question all evening. And I know Ted will be pressing me for answers come Monday morning."

Smiling confidently, Mark reached for her hand and tucked it into the crook of his arm. She tried to pull away, but he wouldn't release his hold. "That's because I don't like mixing business with pleasure. Why ruin a perfectly good evening by discussing business details?"

"But the dinner was to discuss business. I thought I

explained that." Francie's frustration reflected on her face and in her voice.

"So what sort of enticement are you going to give me to get me to sign with your company?"

She ground to a halt and finally managed to free herself from his hold. "Enticement!" Her face turned beet red. "How dare you imply— What sort of woman do you think I am?"

"Hey, wait a minute! I wasn't implying anything sordid. I just want to know what my advantage is in going with your firm, that's all. There are plenty of firms, especially in New York, that would love to have my business."

Her indignation dissolved immediately, though bits of color still stained her cheeks, from embarrassment at jumping to conclusions, no doubt. "Oh. Well, I thought I had explained all that—TV talk shows, book tour, that sort of thing."

"And will you be accompanying me, teaching me the ropes, so to speak? I'm new at this publicity business and will need help from someone who has experience. I won't feel comfortable going it alone." Going on a book tour with Francie held definite possibilities for seduction. Too bad he didn't really have a book.

"Of course Ted and I will be at your disposal, Mark. You needn't worry that we'll abandon you. Ted is very good at—"

"I don't want Ted. I want to work with you exclusively. If you can guarantee that, and if you can promise to humor me in my rather unorthodox requests, then I'll sign with Baxter."

"What sort of unorthodox requests?" Suspicion creased her brows and she looked wary. "I'm not sure I like the sound of that."

"Since we live in such close proximity I thought perhaps we could spend more time getting to know each other. That way you'll be able to construct a publicity campaign that fits my personality, my uniqueness as an author/photographer. You did say that Baxter Promotions was a very hands-on company. I'm only asking that you put your money where your mouth is."

"As long as you understand that our relationship will be strictly business and nothing more. Like you, I don't mix business with pleasure."

"Oh, so you think that being in my company is pleasurable? I'm flattered."

"I didn't say that."

"So you don't think it's pleasurable? Then why do you want me for a client?"

"Will you quit twisting my words, Mark? I just said that I want our relationship to remain businesslike. Sometimes I get the impression that you expect more than that. If I've misread you, then I apologize."

"You haven't misread me. I admit that I'd like to explore the possibility of furthering a relationship with you."

"I'm sorry, Mark, but I don't want a relationship with you, or anyone else, at the moment."

"You seem to have an aversion to the word 'relationship.' Why is that? Have you had an unpleasant experience?"

"That's personal. I don't think it's wise to—"

"Like I said, Francie, I want to get to know you better, as it relates to our doing business together. Those are the terms under which I'll sign your contract. If you refuse, then so will I."

Heaving a defeated sigh, she wrapped her coat more closely around her, as if it could protect her from the unknown. "I've had three engagements, none of which ended in matrimony, so I'm not very good at long-term relationships. There, are you satisfied?"

He did his best to look contrite. "Oh, sorry. I didn't know you got dumped. That must have been tough."

Her face flamed and he almost laughed at her indignation. "I didn't get dumped. I—I'm embarrassed to say that I was the one who did the dumping."

"Well, if those men you were involved with weren't right for you, then you were wise to find that out before the wedding. It would have been far worse if you had gone through with all the exhaustive plans, led the guys down a primrose path, and then discovered you'd made a mistake. As a man, I'm not sure my ego could have taken that. A man's ego is a fragile thing, you know."

"Um, yes, I guess you're right."

Mark could tell Francie was uncomfortable, which was good. He hoped she felt guilty as hell for what she put those poor saps through, including his brother. But he doubted it. And he had no sympathy for her, not after what she'd done to Matt.

"Do you think you'll ever get married?" he asked while they waited for the traffic light to change. "Don't you want to have a family someday?"

Sighing deeply, she shook her head. "I've decided to concentrate on my career. I think I'll be more successful at it than the other."

For some reason Francie's words didn't ring true. "Your mother wants grandchildren. She told me as much. And I think she'd be very disappointed to hear what you've just said."

Francie made a face of disgust. "My mother wants a lot of things, Mark, and she's the biggest part of my three previous problems."

So Matt was just a "problem" her mother had created? Doesn't this woman take responsibility for anything?

"You can't really blame her. All mothers want to be grandmothers, just like most women want to be mothers."

"*Most*, but not all. And what about you? Do you want to get married and have a family?"

"If I meet the right woman, then yes, I'd love to have a family someday. The idea of having a son or daughter thrills me." Which was the absolute truth. But at this juncture in his life, Mark doubted he'd ever have a family, let alone a wife. And the thought pained him.

Her eyes widened. "Really? That's unusual coming from a man like you."

"A man like me?"

"I didn't mean that to be a negative. I just meant that you have a successful career, which seems to be heading off in a whole new direction. Why would you want to compromise that with a family?"

"I can have both. Seeing the world alone isn't as much fun as it's cracked up to be. I'm getting to that point in my life where I want more. Growing old alone holds little appeal."

"You sound like my mother. Are you sure you two haven't been comparing notes?"

Mark grinned. "Quite sure." Not yet, anyway. But that was definitely part of his agenda.

"Have you ever been in love?"

He nodded. "Yes, once. It didn't work out." Which was fortunate, now that he looked back on it. He and Nicole would never have worked, for a multitude of reasons. Perhaps she had sensed that.

"How about you?"

"I told you, I was engaged three—"

"Yes, you did. But you didn't say anything about being in love with any of your fiancés."

Francie thought a moment and a multitude of emotions flitted across her face. "No, I don't think I was in love with any of them. I liked them all, of course. But love?" She shook her head. "I guess that was the biggest part of the problem, and the reason I couldn't go through with the weddings. I bought into the fairy tale about meeting Prince Charming and living happily ever after. But unfortunately it never happened. I'm too much of a realist to think it ever will."

Francie's honesty touched him, in a very disturbing way. He didn't want to think that they might have something in common.

"Sounds to me like you haven't met the right man yet." *And I intend to be that man.* "When you do, you'll open up your heart, just wait and see."

"You sound like a hopeless romantic, Mark. That surprises me."

"I'm a *hopeful* romantic. And why does it surprise you? Don't you think men can have the same depth of feelings as women, want the same things out of a relationship? I bet those men you dumped were crushed, just as you would have been had the shoe been on the other foot."

She had the grace to blush. "I feel terrible about what happened. But what's done is done. It's too late to cry over spilled milk, as my mother is fond of saying. And I'd like to think that I've learned a lot about myself from the experiences I've had."

Yeah, like the fact you're a heartless witch!

Mark was furious with Francie's cavalier attitude. This woman, who looked so sweet and innocent, had ruined three men's lives and all she had to say was that she had learned from it?

"I'm sure the men you dumped don't share your attitude."

"Probably not. But there's nothing I can do about that now, so I choose not to brood over it. I can only hope that I won't make the same mistakes again."

Mark felt an inordinate amount of relief when they finally arrived back at the apartment building. He didn't want to be in Francesca Morelli's company right now, wasn't sure what he'd do to the woman if he was left alone with her.

But strangulation was definitely a possibility.

FRANCIE ALWAYS DREADED Sunday dinner at her parents' house, but even more so today, since finding out that her mother's sister, Florence, would be there.

She'd thought up a hundred excuses why she

couldn't attend, then discarded every one of them, knowing her mother would grill her with the same ruthless determination as a police investigator grilled a murder suspect.

Aunt Flo was Francie's least favorite relative. The woman took great delight in embarrassing her at every turn.

Today was no exception.

"Here comes the bride, all dressed in green. Her grooms were left standing at the altar, isn't she mean?"

"Thank you, Aunt Flo," Francie said, unbuttoning her coat. "It's lovely to see you, too." *Not!* She'd rather be in the company of Attila the Hun. Come to think of it, the similarities were astounding.

The older woman held up a glass of Chianti, as if to toast her niece, but then decided against it and downed it in one gulp.

Nasty old bitch!

"Flo, leave my daughter alone. Francie is a good girl. Hasn't she come to see her mother and father, to pay her respects? A mother is blessed to have a child like that."

Only because I was forced to, Francie thought ungraciously.

"One of these days she'll make a good match and get married. Wait and see," Josephine added.

Florence made a face, then told Francie, "This wedding business is getting fishy. If you're a lesbian, you should just come out and say so. At least we would know where you stand. Of course, your family would disown you. The shame would be too great."

All eyes turned toward Francie and she stiffened. Lisa, who was sitting on the edge of her father's chair, clamped a hand over her mouth, so she wouldn't burst out laughing. Grandma Abrizzi grabbed her cane, giving serious thought to busting her youngest daughter over the head with it.

"I guess I could ask the same of you, Aunt Flo. After all, you've never married. Maybe you've got some skeletons in your closet you haven't told us about. A girlfriend, perhaps?"

Francie's mother's gaze drifted heavenward and she crossed herself, muttering a prayer beneath her breath.

Like a volley at a tennis match, all eyes shifted between the two combatants, landing on a red-faced Florence. "How dare you say such a thing. I am a respectable, God-fearing woman. The love of my life died many years ago, which is why I never married. I remain loyal to his memory. God rest his soul."

"I'm respectable, too—" *well, sort of* "—and if I were a lesbian," Francie stated, ignoring her aunt's bald-faced lie about her mysterious nameless love, "I'd have no problem admitting it. Some of my best friends are gays and lesbians, and I don't like them any less for their choice of lifestyle." In fact, she liked them much better than the woman seated in front of her.

Mark had just arrived and stood in the open doorway, grinning. He'd heard most of the entire exchange and was impressed with the way Francie had held her own with her aunt.

The old woman began cracking her knuckles, a

clear indication of how displeased she was with her niece at the moment. Aunt Flo didn't like to be bested.

"Who are you?" Florence asked Mark when she finally took notice of him. "This is a private family discussion. How did you get in here? Call the police, John."

All heads turned toward the doorway, including Francie, who gasped when she saw who was standing there.

Good grief! Could this day get any worse?

What a stupid question, Francie. You're at your parents' house. Remember?

"What are you doing here?" she asked, her tone accusatory.

"The door was left ajar, so I came in. And to answer your question—I was invited. At least, I thought I was invited. I'm not so sure anymore. And please don't call the police. I'll just leave quietly, if the invitation no longer stands."

Dressed in a pink polyester pantsuit—Josephine hadn't met a polyester garment she didn't like—she bustled forward, rubbing her hands together nervously and smiling apologetically. "Of course you're invited, Mr. Fielding. Come in, come in, and meet the rest of the family." She quickly made the introductions, making sure everyone knew that this was Francie's new *friend*.

Francie's father cast the man a look of pure sympathy, for he knew without a doubt that fiancé number four had been chosen. "Nice to meet you," John said, holding out his hand.

Florence merely grunted when her turn came to be

introduced and refilled her wineglass. "I'm hungry. When do we eat?"

"You'll have to excuse my sister-in-law and daughter," Francie's father added. "I think they're cut from the same cloth."

"Pop! How could you compare me to Aunt Flo? She's nasty to the bone."

Florence, who had moved into the kitchen, didn't hear her niece's last remark, much to Josephine's great relief. Josephine might be opinionated and meddlesome, but Florence was the devil incarnate.

"I invited Mr. Fielding to join us for dinner today, Francie. Why don't you take his coat and make him feel welcome?"

So much for not mixing business with pleasure, and for thinking that her mother wasn't going to play matchmaker.

Naive, Francie. Very naive.

"I'm sorry if I sounded rude, Mark. No one—" she stared meaningfully at her mother, who had the grace to blush "—told me you were coming today." *Or else I would have made up an excuse and stayed home.*

"I don't get that many home-cooked meals, so when your mom phoned and invited me to Sunday dinner, I just couldn't pass up the invitation. Hope you don't mind."

"Not at all," she lied, pasting on a smile and cursing her mother beneath her breath. She'd have a few things to say to the interfering woman later. "My mother is always so...thoughtful. I just hope you know what you're letting yourself in for."

"Francesca, you'll make Mr. Fielding think we are

terrible people," Josephine said with a great deal of indignation.

"We are, Mom." Lisa smiled and wiggled her fingers at Mark. "Welcome. Francie's told me all about you. She said you had eyes the color of sapphires. Guess she was right."

Francie felt the heat rise up her face as it turned three shades of purple. *Please, God, take me now. I'm ready to go.*

Mark grinned. "She's never mentioned that to me, Lisa. And please, everyone, call me Mark."

Francie clamped on to Mark's arm and dragged him toward the living room or "front" room, as her parents called it. "I'm not sure it's a good idea that you came today, Mark. After all, we did agree to keep our relationship strictly business and this isn't exactly in keeping with that."

"Your mom didn't mention that you'd be here today," he lied. "And at any rate, I don't see a difference in having dinner in a restaurant or in a home. We're still eating."

"You'll be sorry you accepted. You don't know what it's like being part of an Italian family. Everyone is outspoken and somewhat rude. They don't mean to be, it's just the way it is. Well, I should say, with the exception of my aunt. She's rude, nasty and she means it."

"I think I can hold my own with Aunt Florence. I've been tested in the battlefield." He grinned and she finally smiled.

"Don't be too sure. Aunt Flo has issues when it comes to men. I don't think she likes them. Come to think of it, I don't think she likes anyone, especially me."

"Dinner's ready," Josephine called from the dining room.

"Are you sure you're up for this? Don't say I didn't warn you."

"I adore large Italian families."

"Then I take it you've never had dinner with one like mine before. Talk about battlefields. You'll feel like you've been put through the ringer by the time my mom and aunt get done with you. You've already been lined up as the next sacrificial lamb. And they do a mean interrogation. The Spanish Inquisition had nothing on those two."

"You mean, lined up for you?"

Francie nodded. "That's exactly what I mean. If you're smart, you'll leave now and spare us both the aggravation. My mom thinks you'll make an excellent groom. She's already given you the Good Housekeeping Seal of Approval. When your back is turned she'll take your measurements and order your tuxedo."

Mark laughed. "Well, it's lucky, then, that I'm quite fond of lamb, isn't it?"

"It's your funeral."

"Don't you mean wedding?"

"Same thing, in my opinion."

8

"GET CHANGED," Leo ordered as soon as Francie walked through the doorway of their apartment, her raincoat dripping onto the green-tiled entryway.

"It's raining like a demon out there. I feel like a drowned rat. I couldn't find a cab and had to walk. I'm not happy with God at the moment. I think He's pissed at me." Just then a boom of thunder exploded, giving credence to her comment. "See? I told you He was pissed."

Grinning widely, Leo, who looked as excited as a kid who'd been gifted with a new toy on Christmas morning, ignored her weather report. She knew her roommate well enough to know that Leo was up to something, and it probably wasn't *something* she was going to like. Surprises were part of her roommate's charm, if you could call it that.

"We're having a party tonight."

"What?" Francie kicked off her new heels, which were soaked down to the soles and killing her feet, and groaned loudly in protest. "But I'm tired. I've been working all day. Some of us do have to work, Leo. And you said nothing about a party when I got home last night, or this morning, for that matter." She shook out her coat, hanging it on the rack near the front door.

Francie felt mentally exhausted. After the horrible dinner at her mother's house last night—no food fights occurred, but verbal slings were tossed—and trying to keep her distance from Mark, which was getting harder with every encounter, then the disagreement she'd had with Ted this morning over the size of Mark's deposit, which Ted didn't think was big enough and she thought quite adequate, Francie was definitely not in a party mood.

"You could have called me at work to let me know about the party. That would have been the polite thing to do."

"I tried. Didn't that airhead of a receptionist give you my message? I told her to write it down."

She shook her head, knowing that Gloria wasn't very efficient when it came to relaying messages, and also knowing that Ted hadn't hired the attractive woman for her efficiency or brains.

"No matter. I really didn't decide about having the party until a few hours ago. But don't worry. I've taken care of everything. The Mexican restaurant down the street, El Gordito's, is going to cater. The food should be here at any moment. It's going to be delish. I've got a guy coming to do the bartending, and the invitations have already been issued via fax, e-mail and phone. It's all taken care of. You won't have to do a thing, except look beautiful."

Francie's face filled with dismay. "But I have nothing to wear." She'd just dropped off a pile of dresses at the cleaner's, so her wardrobe was a bit sparse at the moment, especially when it came to party clothes, not that she had that many to begin with.

Unlike most of her single friends, Francie wasn't a party animal. She didn't like going out every night of the week, preferring instead to stay home and have quiet, intimate evenings with friends, watching a movie or just chatting the night away.

"Who's coming to this shindig of yours, anyway?"

"Ours, sweetie. It's *our* party. And everyone is coming." He put a CD into the player and the room came alive with mariachi music. "I invited all of my friends, some of yours and several of our neighbors."

Neighbors, being the operative word, Francie thought, trying hard not to sway in time to "Celito Lindo," but finding it difficult. She also found it difficult not to physically abuse her roommate.

"Mark's coming to the party, isn't he?" Did Leo never tire of meddling? He was getting to be as bad as her mother, or maybe he was worse. She couldn't really decide.

And it wasn't that she didn't enjoy Mark's company. Quite the opposite, in fact. She enjoyed it too damn much. Being in his company was very addictive. Mark was so different than the other men she had dated—attentive without being fawning, always laughing and finding the humor in every situation. She could definitely get used to being with Mark on a full-time basis.

And therein lay the problem.

"Of course he's invited. I owe him for the camera lessons. And it wouldn't have been very neighborly to exclude him, now would it?"

She heaved a sigh and for the first time noticed the piñata, streamers and colorful decorations that Leo had strung up around the apartment.

Chips, salsa, guacamole dip and other appetizers waited for guests on the coffee and end tables, and a full pitcher of margaritas rested on the dining room table, waiting for unsuspecting revelers. Leo made a mean margarita.

"The apartment looks very festive, Leo, which makes me think you've got too much time on your hands. You need to find a job and work like normal people, instead of sitting around all day, thinking of ways to spend your money."

"If you hurry and change, I'll give your suggestion some thought," he promised, fingers crossed behind his back. "There's a surprise for you on your bed. I hope you like it. When I saw it today I couldn't resist. It was so you."

"You mean, Pierce Brosnan is visiting?"

Leo grinned. "Not quite, sweetie, but close. It's something I thought you could use for the party tonight."

Another gift. Francie sighed. Leo was always buying her presents. And though she appreciated his thoughtfulness and generosity, she wasn't in a financial position to reciprocate, which made her feel bad.

"Thank you, Leo, but you shouldn't spend your money on me. I've told you that before." At his woebegone expression, she suddenly felt petty and finally relented. "But it was very thoughtful of you. I'm sure I'll love whatever it is you've bought me."

"Of course you will. I have excellent taste. And

you're really so easy to buy for. I just thought Catherine Zeta-Jones, and pumped it up a notch."

Good Lord! She should be so lucky to have that woman's face and body. Even when the actress was pregnant, which seemed frequently, she looked better than Francie.

"I want to put on a really good show tonight, don't you?"

Filled with suspicion, Francie's eyes suddenly narrowed. "Is your new boyfriend coming tonight? Is that what this is all about?" It seemed every time Leo found a new friend, he had to celebrate with a party or dinner out. Francie was usually his partner in *dine.*

The blond man grinned. "I just bought this new silk shirt. Isn't it divine? And blue is so my color. I can't wait for Phil to see me in it."

Francie rolled her eyes but the doorbell rang before she could comment, which was very lucky for Leo.

THE WOMAN was proving to be impossible.

Mark wondered if his scheme to lure Francie to the altar was ever going to pan out. She'd turned avoidance into an art form. Lucky for him that Josephine had done her best to throw them together last night or he'd never have made any connection whatsoever.

Not that you could call chitchat in front of the relatives a connection, but it was better than nothing. They had listened to Placido Domingo CDs while sitting on the sofa together, though she hadn't seemed particularly affected by the romantic songs. Of course, her grandmother and mother singing along at the tops of their lungs could have accounted for that.

Cats in heat had more musical ability.

The Morellis were definitely a breed unto their own. They fought with each other such as dogs over a bone, cursed the most inane things, like whether or not sugar should be added to spaghetti sauce, or gravy, as they called it, and laughed at the drop of a hat at inside jokes that apparently had been going on for years.

It was clear they loved each other, but it was definitely in their own way, and not what he was used to.

Mark's family was affectionate, respectful and kind to each other, in both word and deed. They had their share of disagreements, as did most families, but they weren't verbally abusive and they certainly didn't curse one another.

The Fieldings were almost boring by comparison to the Morellis.

It might have been a good thing that Matt had escaped becoming a member of such a volatile family. Mark wasn't sure his little brother would have been up for it, or would have approved of their shenanigans.

Matt was conservative, down to his silk boxer shorts. He was reserved in his dress, almost straitlaced when it came to reputation, public displays of affection, or making a scene; that was the lawyer in him. And hearing Josephine call her sister a "demented old whore" might very well have put him right over the edge.

Francie, on the other hand, seemed to take it all in stride, though she'd had a moment of embarrassment when Grandma Abrizzi had pulled up the skirt of her dress to reveal that her stockings were rolled up with old-fashioned elastic garters. Mark found the outspoken old woman, who felt the need to comment on everything, amusing.

The opportunities for wooing last night had definitely been limited.

Fortunately, Mark would have another chance with Francie this evening, and he intended to make the most of it. Thanks to Leo, he and Ms. Morelli would be thrown together once again. And there wouldn't be many heterosexual men at the party to offer much competition.

There were definite advantages to having a gay male friend, now that he thought about it.

Smiling into the mirror, Mark had just knotted the blue silk tie he'd bought this afternoon when his cell phone rang.

"Hey, bro! How's life treating you?"

Mark was surprised to hear Matt's voice. "I thought you were in Maui with Mom and Dad." If his family had arrived home early, it would ruin everything.

"I am. We're having a pretty nice time, considering what prompted the trip."

He could hear the pain in his brother's voice. Matt was obviously still hurting over Francie, which validated the distasteful job Mark had to do.

He'd had misgivings, given serious thought about chucking the entire scheme. There'd been times when Francie didn't seem to be the heartless witch he thought her to be. But then he remembered how she'd hurt his brother and those other men she obviously cared nothing about, and he knew he had to go through with it.

"Time will make things better, Matt. You'll see."

"I guess. Say, how come you're not in Afghanistan? I wasn't expecting you to answer your cell. I was planning to leave a message, to let you know we were all doing okay."

Unwilling to raise his brother's suspicions, Mark thought quickly. "The assignment ended sooner than I expected, so I came back to Philadelphia. I'll be heading off again in a day or two. I'm just waiting to hear where they're going to send me, probably Iraq, now that things are heating up over there."

"Well, be careful. Mom and Dad are worried about you. It's all they've been talking about. I'm not going to mention Iraq. That would freak them out and spoil their trip."

Mark felt like crap for deceiving his parents. Lying and pretense went against his grain. It was the worst part of this whole fiasco. "I think that's wise. And don't you worry, either, bro. The A.P. has taken every precaution to ensure all of our safety."

"Glad to hear it."

Mark could hear the rhythmic sound of the ocean waves in the background. Matt must have been using his cell phone on or near the beach. "So tell me, Matt, are you enjoying yourself? Got a tan yet?"

"It's beautiful here. If I didn't have a job that I loved so much back in Philadelphia, I'd move here in a heartbeat. It's so relaxing and peaceful and just what I needed to get my mind off…things."

"You can find a position in a law firm in Maui just

as easily as you did here at home. Though I know Mom and Dad would miss you, especially since I'm gone most of the time."

"Yeah, that's one of the reasons I've hesitated to make a move. Mom and Dad aren't getting any younger, and I'd worry about them if I lived so far away."

Matt had shouldered the responsibility for their parents for years, while Mark had traveled the world, doing pretty much what he pleased. Perhaps it was time he did his part in allowing his brother to spread his wings. The change would be good for Matt, and maybe for him, too. Mark had been rootless for too long.

"Once this next job is done I'm thinking about asking for assignments closer to home. Perhaps then, you can think about making the move you want, to wherever you want."

Excitement filled Matt's voice. "If you're serious, then I'll definitely give the idea of relocation some thought, perhaps check into a few firms while I'm here. Putting distance between myself and Philadelphia appeals to me at the moment."

"Do it, bro. I'm serious." Mark was only sorry he'd waited so long to make the offer.

"So, have you been haunting your old hangouts since you've been back? Bars are great places to find women. I hope you've had the opportunity to meet some," Matt stated.

Mark felt another twinge of guilt. "Just one, but she's no one I want to get involved with on a permanent basis."

"You're smart. I'm going to remain a bachelor. It's much safer and far less painful than having your heart broken. I finally figured that out, though it took me a while."

Mark felt relieved and sad at the same time. It was never pleasant to have your illusions shattered.

They chatted for a few more minutes, then Mark set down his cell phone and looked in the mirror. The man who stared back was handsome, suave and filled with purpose. He knew what he had to do, and he was going to do it.

"You haven't got a chance, Francie, honey. I'll make you beg for it before this night is through."

FRANCIE STARED at her reflection in the full-length mirror nailed to her closet door and felt like crying.

The wine-red dress was gorgeous, but way too tight. Leo had purchased a size eight instead of a ten. She felt like a stuffed sausage. Every lump of cellulite she owned showed, and her boobs, which were usually not a consideration, were out there, in a major way.

Okay, so Dolly Parton had nothing to fear, but Francie felt downright stacked.

"How am I going to wear this dress in front of Mark?" she asked her reflection, sighing deeply. "He'll think I'm making a move on him. And that's the last impression I want to give." First her grandmother bares her bony knees to the man, and now Francie was going to hang her boobs in his face.

Mark was going to think that the women of her

family were all sex crazed. In truth, they were just crazed.

Not that she gave a damn about what he thought, but still...

Not wearing the dress would hurt Leo's feelings, and she couldn't do that. The man was sensitive about such things and was likely to pout for days afterward. "Damn, I'm screwed either way!"

The upside was that, lumps aside, she looked pretty good. The silk dress came to mid-thigh and the sheer black Donna Karan nylons made her legs—one of her best features—look sexy, not to mention firm, which would make up for her non-firm butt.

Catherine Zeta-Jones wouldn't be losing any sleep over Francesca Morelli, unfortunately.

"THERE YOU ARE, sweetie," Leo said when Francie entered the already crowded living room. "My, but you look fabulous. Doesn't Francie look gorgeous, Phil?" he asked his companion.

Leo's new friend gave her the once-over, smiled a fake smile, which made Francie dislike him instantly, and nodded. It was obvious that fake-ass Phil, which she now decided to call him, wasn't quite as impressed with her appearance as the blue-eyed man now sauntering over in her direction, looking as if he could devour her in one huge bite.

Speaking of which—

Mark looked yummy. Spread that man with chocolate and whipped cream and I could eat him for—

"Hello, Mark. I wasn't expecting to see you again

so soon." He grinned in response and she nearly fell over on her spiked heels.

And what was that delicious aftershave he was wearing?

Warning: implosion imminent!

"Wow! Terrific dress. You look quite different tonight, Ms. Morelli. Hot comes to mind."

He winked and she blushed down to the toes of her Jimmy Choo shoes. "Thank you. I'm glad to see that you survived my family."

"I liked them. Well, maybe not Aunt Flo, she was a bit hard to take, but everyone else was great." Reaching over, he lifted two margaritas off the tray on the side table and handed her one.

"Well, if you didn't like my aunt, then I'd say that you definitely have good taste."

He gazed at her lips and she warmed instantly. "I like to think so."

The salt on the rim of the frosty glass was going to add five pounds of water to Francie's weight by morning, but right now she didn't care. Right now she needed fortification, and some cooling off. Mark made her hot, with a capital H! She took a huge gulp, which rendered the glass half empty, much to her surprise.

Mark's brow shot up. "You must have been thirsty. Careful. That tequila can go right to your head."

"I am. I've been rushing around since I got home to the news that we were having a party tonight. Leo neglects to mention these things sometimes. And don't worry about the margaritas. I can drink them with no problem. In fact, I've never had a hangover, not once in my life."

"Wish I could say the same. I've had some whoppers." Mark's gaze floated across the room, to where Francie's roommate was singing in a falsetto voice, along with Barry Gibb of the Bee Gees, to "Staying Alive" from *Saturday Night Fever.* The recent Broadway musical revival had given the old movie a resurgence in popularity.

Leo looked happy and relaxed, and Mark envied him that. "Leo's in his element tonight, that's for certain."

There were perhaps three dozen people crammed into the apartment, all laughing and singing and having a great time.

"He's never met a party he didn't like. Leo's the most extroverted extrovert I've ever met."

"I admire him for it. I'm not as outgoing as I'd like to be. Guess my job's made me a solitary sort." Mark handed Francie another margarita, which she took and began sipping.

"Speaking of your job, I need to get a copy of your upcoming book, or at least be able to take a look at some of your photography, to get an idea of how we're going to proceed with your campaign."

Mark's eyes lit. "Why not come—"

"Francie, there you are!" Joyce, who had just arrived on the arm of Eddie Bertucci, sidled up next to her friend and kissed her on the cheek. She was wearing tight black leather pants and a fuzzy gold angora sweater. "You look fabulous! My God! Where did you get that dress? It's too sexy for words."

"I totally concur," Mark said, holding out his hand as he introduced himself. Francie felt a glow from within.

"Ah, the neighbor. I've heard a lot about you. Leo and Lisa have been singing your praises and talking nonstop about the new man in Francie's life." Joyce grinned at her friend.

Francie scowled. "Joyce, really!" But for some reason, probably the alcohol, she was unable to hold it long and burst out laughing.

Sniffing the air a few times, Francie said, "Hi, Eddie," then began laughing hysterically again. The man stared back as if she were nuts.

"What did you put in Francie's drink, Mark?" Joyce asked. "You haven't been spiking her margaritas with Ruffies, have you?"

Mark's cheeks filled with color.

"Don't mind Joyce," Eddie said, casting his girlfriend a disgusted look. "She always says whatever's on the top of her head, and it's usually stupid."

"Who do you think you're calling stupid, you smelly pig," Joyce retorted, turning on her heel and crossing the room in quick strides, Eddie close on her heels.

"Wait, baby! I didn't mean it," he shouted after her.

Mark grinned. "Uh-oh, trouble in paradise. Even your friends are volatile. Is it the neighborhood or just hot Italian blood?"

Francie, feeling no pain, finished off her drink and grabbed another margarita from the table behind her. "Joyce speaks her mind. And Eddie is only a temporary play toy. He's promised to take her to see *Mama*

Mia, so she's stringing him along. I hope he doesn't take her, so she and I can go, like we'd originally planned." It was a selfish thought, but a truthful one, Francie thought.

"I've got two tickets to see *Mama Mia*. Would you like to go with me?" Mark offered.

Francie's eyes widened at the invitation. Well, as wide as they could open, considering the upper lids felt as if they'd been glued to the bottom ones. "I didn't know you liked musicals. You never said."

He laughed. "There's a lot about me you don't know. I love musicals, and Abba is one of my favorite groups."

"Me, too! What a coincidence. I guess there's more to you than I originally thought. And we really need to rect...recti...fix that part about me getting to know you better, if I'm going to be working with you."

"I totally agree. Why don't we dart over to my apartment and I'll show you some of what I've been working on, then we can make arrangements to see the play."

Francie hesitated momentarily, biting her lower lip, but the alcohol had all but obliterated her reservations, and she grinned, somewhat lopsidedly. "Is that sort of like inviting me over to see your sketchings?"

Mark wiggled his brows in a dastardly fashion. "You've found me out, Miss Morelli. So are you coming?"

Mmm. What a delicious thought.

"Stop it!"

"Stop what? I wasn't doing anything, Francie."

"I wasn't talking to you."

"Should I be frightened?"

"Yes, very." She slipped her arm through his, margarita glass and all. "Shall we, Mr. Fielding?"

"Indeed, Ms. Morelli. We shall."

9

ENTERING MARK'S APARTMENT, Francie was filled with a great deal of trepidation. She was breaking her own rule and, somewhere in her befuddled mind, she knew that. But she couldn't get her body to cooperate with what her brain was trying to communicate. The "Run, Francie, run" mantra was not currently playing inside her head—*Where was a good mantra when you needed one?*—and that had her worried big-time.

She was hopelessly attracted to Mark, and she knew that attraction could only get her into trouble.

Big-time!

"So where are these photographs of yours?" she asked.

"I hate to sound like a cliché, but would you believe, in the bedroom?" Mark answered with a devilish grin that she found way too appealing.

Damn! She really sucked at avoidance.

Double damn that he was so darn cute!

Double, double damn that she was so wishy-washy!

Disgusted with herself, Francie shook her head and immediately regretted the motion, though she wasn't about to admit that the tequila was doing a number on her brain cells, her now *dead* brain cells. Not after she'd bragged that alcohol had no effect on her.

Ha! Ha! Ha! That was a good one.

"It's not very original. But I'll give you points for trying," she finally said.

"I actually use the spare bedroom as a gallery of sorts. I didn't want to rent furniture for the room, since I won't be having any guests staying overnight, so I set up my computer and office in there. The white walls make a nice backdrop for the black-and-white photos, if I do say so myself."

Francie followed Mark toward the back of the apartment. His bedroom door was open and she could see that his room wasn't quite as neat as the rest of the flat. The bedspread and blankets were mussed, the pillow dented, looking as if he'd taken a brief nap before coming to the party. There were clothes strewn on the carpeted floor and the chair by the bed. A pair of black silk boxers dangled from the doorknob.

A tingling feeling started in the pit of her stomach, radiating down to her toes. Thinking that Mark had actually lain in that bed, probably naked, sent her hormones into overdrive. Good Lord! She was having a hot flash and she wasn't even thirty yet.

What on earth is the matter?

As if you don't know.

She was primed and ready for ignition. All she needed was a spark to set her off.

Turning his head, the *spark* looked back at her and asked almost the same question. "What is it? Is something wrong? You look rather odd."

Fighting the urge to groan, she shook her head.

"Nothing's wrong. I talk to myself sometimes. You'll get used to it. And I always look odd, it's part of my charm." She forced a smile, trying to appear pretty and witty, but failing miserably.

"Take care you don't start answering, or you'll really be in trouble."

Too late!

Entering the small bedroom, Francie was immediately entranced by the framed photographs on the walls. They hung uniformly, covering every inch of bare space, and were of excellent quality. You didn't have to be a photography expert to see that Mark was extremely talented.

Slowly she moved from one to the other, noting the pathetic faces of undernourished African children, exotic half-naked Polynesian women, and the bodies of the dead, left on battlefields from various wars fought in faraway lands.

"These are very moving," she said, a lump forming in her throat, which she massaged with her hand. "You have quite a gift for capturing the heart and soul of a person. That one, of the small child with the distended belly, is particularly heart-wrenching.

"I don't think I could do what you do. I wouldn't have the stamina, the guts to face what you have to face to get these kinds of shots."

His eyes reflected surprise at her comments. "Thank you. I rarely share these photographs with anyone. They're among my favorites and are not for sale or public consumption."

"You have a sensitive side, Mark, that is clearly revealed in your work. I already know you're a romantic, but I never realized until now what a sensitive soul you have." She waved toward the wall of photographs. "It's there on display, revealing a part of you that is special and unique."

Her publicist's brain was already conjuring up possibilities to utilize those qualities. The media ate up compassion and sensitivity, probably because they didn't have much of their own.

Moving toward her, Mark held out his hands and pulled Francie to him before she could object. "You're very special, too," he said in a low, sexy voice that made her heart thump madly in her chest and her toes curl downward. "I hope you know that. And I'm honored that you like my work. You have great insight."

"I—" She never got to finish her sentence because Mark's lips captured hers and she lost herself in his kiss—*his very fabulous kiss!*—wrapping her arms about his waist and pulling him closer to her.

His lips were soft and insistent, and when his tongue entered her mouth, and she felt the rhythmic in and out motion, it was all she could do to maintain her equilibrium.

The *"Wow!"* factor was tremendous.

Her insides turned to mush instantly. Her heart raced at such a high rate of speed she felt breathless and unsteady. And the hard member pressing against her belly gave her a good indication that Mark was feeling the same way.

Arousal was a "hard" thing for a man to hide.

When Mark finally released her, Francie felt as if her world had been rocked on its axis. She'd never been kissed like that before, never felt what she'd just felt.

And it scared the hell out of her.

"I think I should go."

He took her hand and caressed it. "Don't go. I won't kiss you again, if you don't want me to. But I won't apologize, either. Because I've wanted to do that from the first moment I set eyes on you."

Yeah, me, too.

Francie smiled ruefully. "That's the problem. I wasn't offended, and I may want you to do it again, and that very fact frightens me."

"Why does it frighten you that a man finds you desirable?"

"I don't know."

But she did.

Francie couldn't afford to get involved with Mark. He was the kind of man she could fall head over heels in love with. Hell, maybe she had already; she didn't know. She was certainly not an expert when it came to matters of the heart, that was for damn certain! Pursuing a relationship would be a disaster, just like all the other disasters she'd had in the past. And she'd promised herself that she wouldn't make the same mistakes again.

Damn it! Why did he have to have an M name?

It was a bad omen.

Mark led her into the living room and they sat on the sofa. "I won't deny that I want you, Francie, but I won't ask for more tonight. I don't take advantage of women who've had too many margaritas, despite their claim to the contrary." He smiled indulgently and she felt her face grow hot.

"That's not my style. When we make love—and we will, rest assured of that—I want you to feel it down to your toes."

Francie should have been upset with Mark's cocky, self-assured attitude that said she was his for the taking, but she couldn't muster up enough indignation. For some stupid reason, she was flattered.

And maybe that was because she not only felt *it* in her toes, but several other spots, too. If the throbbing between her legs didn't stop, she was going to embarrass herself by jumping him first.

"The margaritas went straight to my head," she said by way of explanation, crossing one leg over the other and trying not to squirm.

Or was it his kisses that had drugged her with such desire? She couldn't be sure.

"I know you have set rules about dating clients and all that, but I'm hoping you'll break them for me. I want you to go to the play with me. The tickets are for Saturday night. Will you go?"

She released the breath she didn't know she'd been holding and nodded, knowing without a doubt that their coming together would be inevitable. She'd been waiting for someone to knock her socks off. Well, here he was.

Socks, shoes, the whole enchilada.

"Yes, I'd love to," she finally replied, then backed off a bit. "I mean, we did say that we had to get to know each other better, for the publicity campaign and all, right?"

"Right."

"And I've been dying to see *Mama Mia*. And it would be rude not to accept a client's invitation. And—"

Leaning forward, he kissed the tip of her nose, which she found very endearing. "I'll take you whatever way I can get you."

Naked, with two cherries on—

"I'd better be getting back to the party. Are you coming?"

"No. I don't think I can trust myself around you right now. Tell Leo I've got a headache."

"Hey, that's usually my excuse." Francie grinned, then got up and walked toward the door, wondering if Saturday night could come soon enough, and worrying that it would.

"WHERE HAVE YOU BEEN? I've been waiting for you for over an hour. Leo said you were at the party and then you just disappeared without a word to anyone. I was starting to get worried."

Francie fought the urge to smooth down her hair, which probably looked as though she'd just gotten out of bed—close, but no cigar!

"What are you, my keeper, Lisa? And what are you doing here anyway? Leo didn't tell me you were coming."

"Leo invited me. It is a party, isn't it? And I am your sister, aren't I? In fact, why didn't *you* invite me? I was rather hurt that you didn't. I always invite you to my parties."

"You never have any parties."

"Well, I would, if I did."

Francie sighed. "I didn't know we were having a party until I got home this evening, that's why I didn't invite you. Leo just sprang this on me. I guess he figured that I couldn't say no if I didn't know about it in advance."

Leo was sneaky like that.

"That still doesn't explain where you've been."

Noting several interested and totally inebriated onlookers, Joyce included, Francie grabbed her sister's hand, waved and smiled at her friends, then dragged Lisa into the bedroom, pulling her down beside her on the bed.

"If you must know, I was down the hall at Mark's apartment. And I wish you wouldn't broadcast my personal business in front of the whole room. You know how indiscreet Joyce is. She'll start spreading rumors, truth or no truth. She can't help herself. I love her, but the woman's got a bigger mouth on her than a hippo."

Lisa's brow arched. "Anything you care to confess? You look a bit *messed* with."

Francie's face flared bright enough to match her dress. "Mark kissed me. And that's all he did. I went over to his apartment to look at his photographs, for the campaign that we're working on. Nothing more happened. Oh, except that he invited me to see *Mama Mia* on Saturday night. I can't wait. I'm really looking for—"

"In New York City?" Lisa interrupted, shaking her head, a look of total disbelief on her face.

"You don't seem very pleased about my date. Why

is that? I thought you liked Mark. You seemed to at dinner last night."

"Think, Francie. New York City. That means you'll have to stay overnight. The play probably doesn't start until eight o'clock. It'll run for two or three hours, you'll have a late dinner, maybe take a romantic ride through Central Park, and then..." Lisa left the rest unsaid, but Francie picked up the thread right away and paled slightly.

"Oh, shit! I hadn't thought of that. Well, I'm sure we'll be able to drive or take the train back to Philly after we're done. I don't intend to spend the night with Mark Fielding. I'm not a glutton for punishment, contrary to what you may think. And I'm not *that* easy."

Well, at least not on a first date.

And being easy was relatively subjective anyway.

If a person wanted to have sex, for purely self-indulgent reasons, then what was wrong with that? I mean, she and Mark were two consenting adults. It wouldn't be a crime or anything.

And if they used protection, then so much the—

Shut the hell up, Francie! Just shut the hell up.

"Hey, if you want to have sex with the guy, that's up to you," Lisa said, as if reading Francie's mind. "But I sort of got the impression from what you've said that you weren't ready for another relationship. Of course, I would, if it were me. He's cute, and sexy as hell. You'd be a fool not to, in my opinion."

"Well, nobody's asking for your opinion. I've got enough problems with Mom, without adding sex into the equation. It's clear she's designated Mark as the next fiancé candidate. I should just move to Alaska and be done with it. That's probably the only way she'll ever leave me alone."

"What? And miss all the wonderful plans Mom is making for your next wedding. Besides, she probably knows a lot of Eskimos," Lisa added with a grin.

Fear shot straight through Francie's heart. "What have you heard—about wedding plans, I mean?"

A mysterious look flashed across her sister's face, and Francie grew instantly alarmed. "Nothing," Lisa replied.

"Come on, Lisa, fess up."

"I swear. I haven't heard anything. It's just the way she talks about Mark. I think you're in serious trouble this time, France. Mom is crazy about the guy. She never stops talking about how handsome he is, how much money he makes, what beautiful children you two are going to have. Should I go on?"

Francie shook her head, feeling somewhat nauseated, and she didn't think it had a thing to do with the margaritas she'd consumed.

"You're going to have a tough time getting her to let go of this one, if that's your intention. It's true, she was very interested in the undertaker, but this time is different, Mom's motives are different. I'm not saying pure, just different."

"I've already explained to Mark about Mom and her wedding fetishes. He's cool with it, I think."

"And?"

"He likes her, likes the whole family, if you can believe that."

By the astonished look on Lisa's face, Francie figured she couldn't. "Really? Even Aunt Flo?"

"Well, maybe not her. But you can't blame him. Nobody likes Aunt Flo, even her own mother." Grandma Abrizzi was always bemoaning the fact that the Catholic church didn't approve of birth control.

"So what are you going to do?"

Francie heaved a dispirited sigh. "I suppose suicide is out of the question."

Lisa wrapped a comforting arm around her sister's shoulders. "Don't talk stupid, France. You've just got to beat Mom at her own game. What if you were to tell her how crazy you are about Mark, that you're seriously considering marrying him?"

Francie's eyes rounded and her jaw nearly dropped to her chest before she replied, "Are you crazy? That's just what she wants to hear. I'll be playing right into her hands."

"Not necessarily." Lisa went on to explain. "Mom is thrilled by the hunt, by pushing you into relationships that you don't really want. Maybe she'll lose interest, or even try and dissuade you, if she thinks you're truly interested in marrying Mark. I mean, where would the fun be in that for her?"

"I don't think so, Lisa. It's too risky. Besides, I've already told her I have no intention of getting married. I was quite clear on the subject, adamant even."

"And what did she say?"

"She blew me off, as usual."

"Well, don't blame me when you're being fitted for

wedding dress number four. She bought three new bridal magazines the other day."

"Oh...my...God! The woman is incorrigible. I'm going to have a talk with Dad, ask him to talk some sense into her. This has to be costing him a small fortune. Maybe I can appeal to him on a financial basis. I already tried that with Mom, but she didn't seem to care."

"Are you surprised? When did she ever care about spending Dad's money?"

"Maybe you should talk to her, Lisa. After all, she's spending all of your inheritance on my weddings."

"Good. Then she won't have any money left to spend on mine. I know I'm next, after she marries you off."

"Maybe we should talk to the priest. Father Scaletti might be able to reason with her."

"And lose money he could make for the church?" Lisa shook her head. "Unlikely. The guy is cleaning up on these weddings of yours. Mom and Dad are a gold mine for him."

"I'm doomed. Josephine Morelli is going to haunt me for the rest of my days."

"There is one way you could get Mom off your back. Well, actually two, but the last one is a bit drastic and should be saved for only a dire emergency."

"What are they? I'm desperate and likely to try anything that might work."

"The first one is the most obvious—you could actually get married."

Francie frowned deeply. "That is not a choice, and it's out of the question. What's the other one?"

"You could convince her that you're a lesbian. That way, you'd have an excellent excuse for not wanting to get married. Aunt Flo has already opened the door on that one. All you need do is walk through it."

"A lesbian, huh? Let me give that idea some thought. It's a bit more palatable than the first. Hmmm. Let's see—I'll be kicked out of the family and will be able to live the rest of my life in peace and solitude. It definitely has merit."

Lisa burst out laughing, then Francie followed suit, though she knew that none of what Lisa had said was a laughing matter, especially since she was going to have to give both ideas some serious consideration. And soon.

10

GAZING INTO HIS CUP of hot coffee the following morning, the steam rising up to tickle his nose and make his mouth water, Mark couldn't stop thinking about Francie, who also made his mouth water.

Dammit!

The dark, rich coffee was of a similar color as her curly hair, the heat warming his hands felt like the warmth of her body when he'd pulled her into his arms and kissed her passionately the previous night.

And he was worried.

His thoughts weren't centered on revenge at the moment, but on Francie's comments about his work—the way she'd been able to peer into his soul and offer such amazing insight, as though she really cared about what he was doing. He thought about the way her lips felt, soft and pliant, beneath his when his mouth devoured hers, the silky feel to her skin when he caressed her and—

"Shit!"

What the hell was the matter with him?

Listen to yourself! You're besotted with the woman, like a high school kid with a hard-on.

Maybe this was the same spell Francie had cast over his brother and the other men she'd been involved with. After all, she'd had plenty of practice and probably had seduction and sensuality down to a science—a pint-size femme fatale who wreaked havoc wherever she went.

And here he was about to fall under whatever magic charm she had cast over him, make the same mistakes as all the other "victims" she'd lured into her web of deceit and desire.

But he wouldn't.

Mark was too smart for that.

And he'd been burned too many times to be careless.

He was determined to stick to the original plan to woo, bed and *almost* wed the dishonest woman, then make the big skeedaddle before Francie knew what hit her.

But he wouldn't take as much pleasure in doing it now.

Not now that he'd kissed her.

"THANKS FOR MEETING ME, Pop. I know you usually mow the lawn on Saturday morning, so I appreciate your taking time out of your busy day to come and talk with me." Francie almost choked on the word "busy," because that was stretching things a wee bit.

Her father was the most laid-back man she knew. Sometimes you had to take a mirror to his nose just to see if he was still breathing.

Mowing the lawn was his Saturday ritual. First, he ate a huge breakfast, lovingly prepared for him by Josephine. Then he mowed the lawn and performed other yardwork before finally plopping himself in front of the TV for the rest of the afternoon. A beer and a bag of chips by his side, he watched whatever sports program was on, football being his favorite. Though if push came to shove, he'd watch ice dancing with just as much enthusiasm.

"I need to talk to you about something very important. It's sort of an emergency situation."

Dressed in a New York City fireman's T-shirt and hat that he'd bought as a show of support after 9-11, Francie's father looked as though he could handle any emergency situation with ease.

John Morelli gazed at his surroundings and made a face of disgust. "Why did we have to meet here? I don't like this deli. Manny uses too much mustard on the Ruebens. It ruins the whole taste. There are much better places to have breakfast or lunch."

"I'll ask Manny to cut back on the mustard when we order, Pop." *Like that was a major issue,* Francie thought, fighting the urge to roll her eyes.

But she was grateful her father had agreed to meet her this morning on such short notice. Fortunately, it was Josephine's day to get her hair done at the beauty parlor, so she wouldn't get suspicious.

Her mother had worn the same hairstyle for as long as Francie could remember. She wasn't sure what to call it, but Maureen, the seventy-year-old "stylist"—she used that term loosely—used rollers and gobs of hairspray to achieve that football helmet effect her mom was so fond of.

Aside from doing something creative with her own hair, Francie had a million things to accomplish before getting ready for her date with Mark tonight.

Shaving her legs was at the top of her priority list—
they were looking a bit simian at the moment. But she
knew she'd never be able to concentrate on the play
or enjoy her evening with him, if she didn't get this
wedding business resolved.

And she needed her dad's help to do that.

"Maybe I'll order a meatball or sausage sub. Then I
don't have to worry about the mustard," her father
said, his thoughts still centered on his stomach, which
had turned into a full-blown paunch over the years.

She patted his hand, mostly to gain his attention.
When there was food around, her father's mind wan-
dered. Most older men noticed attractive, well-built
women, but not John Morelli, who much preferred to
view a well-stuffed sausage or a thin slice of pros-
cuitto.

"Pop, you've got to do something about Mom.
She's starting to make plans again for another wedding. Lisa told me she's been buying bridal magazines and talking to caterers and florists. You've got
to put your foot down this time and tell her no. I'm at
my wit's end."

Heaving a sigh, her father looked apologetic,
which didn't bode well. "I've tried talking to your
mother, Francie, but she's already made up her mind
that you and Mark are perfect for each other and
should get married. She told me to butt out when I
tried to reason with her."

Like reason was a possibility!

"I'm sorry," he continued, "but I don't think I can
be of much help to you. You know what Josephine is

like when she gets these notions in her head. It's a waste of time and breath when she gets like this."

"I don't want to get married. I told her that, but she just ignores me." Francie had the sudden urge to crawl into her father's lap and bawl.

"Your mother has a one-track mind when it comes to your happiness, Francie. She wants you to get married, settle down and have children. She won't be content until you do. I can't change her mind. She's a stubborn woman, your mother, always has been. But what's a man to do? I love her, God bless her stubborn hide."

"Maybe you could cut off her money and charge cards, then Mom wouldn't be able to arrange another wedding."

Or lock her in a closet for a few years. That would work, too.

"I threatened to do that very thing, said I wouldn't give her any more money to pay for these weddings, that they were costing me a small fortune."

Hope blossomed in Francie's chest and she leaned forward. "And what did she say?"

"That she'd divorce me if I did. Josephine told me that I wasn't being a good husband or father to have such an uncaring attitude about my own daughter's happiness. She also told me I was cheap. Can you believe that, after I bought her those expensive dishes she's been wanting? Now I'm cheap."

"Maybe you could talk to Father Scaletti, ask him to counsel Mom about interfering in her children's lives. Surely there's something in the Bible that covers such things. Thou shalt not ruin your daughter's life. You know, something along those lines."

"That wouldn't do any good. Those two are in cahoots together. He's a priest, for chrissake! It's his job to marry off the whole world and get children for the church. I think he must make a bonus on every baby he baptizes. We got four or five coming in every Sunday. It's a racket, I tell you."

This was not a very encouraging discussion. Matters were going from bad to worse, so Francie decided it was time to pull out all the stops, even if it meant shocking her father.

"Lisa thinks I should tell Mom that I'm a lesbian. I think her idea has merit. What do you think, Pop?"

"Are you? You said the other night at dinner that you weren't. Is there something you want to tell me? It's said that confession is good for the soul, Francie, so maybe you should get it off your chest and be done with it." He closed his eyes, as if the admission would be too difficult to hear.

"I'm not a lesbian. But I could pretend to be and get Mom off my back."

Reaching out, John released the breath he'd been holding and squeezed his daughter's hand. "It's not a good idea, Francie. And I'm not at all surprised that your sister is the one who came up with it. That girl marches to the beat of her own drum, and the tune is quite different from the one the rest of the world plays."

It was true that Lisa was somewhat of a nonconformist, especially when it came to the men she dated—the word "freaks" came to mind—but sometimes, as in this case, she had some good ideas, albeit a wee bit unorthodox.

"It makes perfect sense to me. Aunt Flo has already mentioned it and—"

John shook his head. "No, Francie! That would break your mother's heart. Even more than you not getting married. I couldn't allow you to do that. I know you're a grown woman, and can do pretty much what you please, but in this instance I would not be on your side.

"Telling lies never did anyone any good. I've told you that since you were a little girl. Honesty isn't the best policy—"

"It's the only one," Francie finished on a sigh, knowing he was right.

"Exactly. I'm glad you paid attention all those years to what I was saying."

"But Mom doesn't listen to the truth, Pop. I told her that I don't have any intention of getting married, to Mark or anyone else. But she doesn't seem to hear what I say.

"I can't live my life like this anymore. She's making me nuts. If she doesn't get off my back, I may have to enter a convent." The false admission made her father smile.

"Your mother and I couldn't afford a big wedding when we got married," John tried to explain for the tenth time in at least as many months. "She's trying to live vicariously through you, to experience all the things that she missed. I feel responsible for that, but at the time we got married no one had the money for a fancy wedding party, least of all me.

"I'm sorry you have to bear the brunt of her missing out on all that."

The urge to whine was too strong and Francie indulged. "It's not fair that I'm the one who has to suffer. I love Mom, and I've tried to placate her over the years, by going along with her schemes in an effort to make her happy—which, as you know, is virtually impossible—and by allowing her to foist unsuitable men on me. But I won't do it again. I can't. If she disowns me, then so be it."

John reached out and patted his daughter's cheek, as he'd done a thousand times before. "Your mother would never disown you. Maybe she loves you too much. That's most likely the problem.

"And what about this Mark you brought over to the house? He doesn't seem unsuitable. And the man appears to genuinely care about you. In fact, he told your mother that he was crazy about you."

Francie's mouth fell open. "He did?" The idea that Mark would say such a thing to her mother, especially after knowing what Josephine was like, and the fact that she was looking for a groom, was nothing short of startling. Not to mention flattering.

Of course, it was scary, too!

What if the man was deranged, and she just hadn't realized it yet? Let's face it, he got along with her mother. And that was too weird for words.

"You are so determined not to make a match that maybe you aren't seeing what is right before your eyes, *cara.* I think you like this Mark more than you let on. What do you think?"

Francie thought a moment before answering. "I do like him, but he's a client. I don't think—"

"Lisa told me you have a date with him tonight. Is that so?"

"Yes." Francie felt her cheeks warm. "Lisa has a big mouth. What else did she tell you?"

"Nothing. Is there something else I should know?"

"Just that I feel conflicted about the whole situation. I know I shouldn't be dating a client, but I couldn't seem to say no when Mark asked me out." And that fact alone should have sent up a big, fat, red flag.

The problem was that Francie could picture them together, as a couple—a *copulating* couple!

He arched his right brow. "And you don't find that significant?"

Hell yes! But Francie wasn't about to admit that to her father. "I don't know. I'm not going to read any more into this situation than I have already, and you shouldn't, either. Mark and I are friends, nothing more."

Of course, the kiss they'd shared felt a lot more than friendly. Exchanging spit and mating tongues wasn't usually part of the "friend" equation. But she wasn't going to tell her father that, either.

"You're a grown woman, Francie. I know you know your own mind. Just don't make it up too quickly. You need to take time and think about things. Don't do something just to spite your mother. She loves you and only wants what is best for you."

"I know, Pop, but—"

"But nothing. Let's eat. I didn't have my pancakes and eggs this morning and I'm starving."

Francie heaved a defeated sigh, knowing there'd be no help from this quarter today. And wondering if maybe her sister had been right. Maybe she should just get married and get it over and done with.

If Mark was really interested...

"No!" She banged her fist down on the table, almost upsetting their water glasses and nearly making her father jump out of his seat.

"No? No, what? I didn't say anything."

"It's nothing, Pop. I was just thinking out loud."

"And the answer was no?"

"Yes. No. I mean, yes, it was definitely no."

I'm staying single!

SEATED IN A COZY Italian restaurant on West 46th Street, near Broadway, surrounded by the delicious smells of garlic and basil wafting from the kitchen, and the lilting sound of a pair of strolling violin players, Francie couldn't keep her toe from tapping in time to the show music that still played in her head.

"I think *Mama Mia* has to be my favorite musical production of all time. I just loved it! It was funny, romantic, and the music—Abba's music was too fabulous for words.

"Thank you, for taking me, Mark."

Sipping his glass of Chianti, Mark waited for the tuxedo-garbed waiter, who was most likely an aspiring or out-of-work actor, to stop grinning and set down their slices of cheesecake, thinking there were a few other places he'd like to take the beautiful woman, like to bed.

The scent of her perfume had been driving him crazy all evening, not to mention that she looked damn good in that red leather skirt and black lace top she was wearing.

"I'm glad you enjoyed it. So did I. And I doubt I would have gone, if you hadn't agreed to go with me. Although I like musicals, when I think about going to them it seems like such a girl thing to do."

Francie laughed. "A typical male reaction." She then added, "I don't think I've ever eaten dinner quite this late before. I have absolutely no chance of getting rid of any of these cheesecake calories. They'll go straight to my hips. But it's worth it.

"My mom makes a very good cheesecake, but it's not as good as this. Don't you dare tell her I said that, or I'll never hear the end of it."

"My lips are sealed." Glancing at his Tag Hauer wristwatch, Mark noted that it was almost twelve o'clock. "Do you turn into a pumpkin at the stroke of midnight?" he asked. "Is that why you're worried about the time?"

Francie's smile lit her dark eyes. Bedroom eyes, some would call them—dark, mysterious and very sexy. "No, I turn into the ugly stepmother and big warts grow all over my nose."

He swallowed his smile. "Impossible. Your features are much too perfect. You could never play that role. I was thinking more of Cinderella, the fair damsel in distress who is waiting for her prince charming to come along."

"There's that romantic streak in you again. Careful you don't allow it to get you into trouble."

He gazed into her eyes. "Too late for that, Francie."

She blushed, quite charmingly, Mark thought, as if it were a truly genuine response. But how could that be? She was used to dating and discarding. Francie didn't know how to form lasting relationships. He wasn't sure she wanted to, judging by her track record.

No, Francie was fickle, just like all the other women he'd known.

It was too bad, because he liked her. He hadn't at first, but now that he'd gotten to know her, he really did find her enchanting and likable.

Not that it would do him much good. He still had his plan to implement—he might like her, but he didn't trust her. And there was also the matter of his younger brother.

Even if he wanted to form a relationship with Francie, Matt would always stand in his way. And Mark would never do anything to hurt his brother, especially not over a woman.

"You look so serious. Is something the matter?"

Shaking his head, Mark smiled. "Just thinking. I don't say my thoughts out loud, like you do."

"That's probably a good thing. I'm not sure I'd want to know what you're thinking, especially when you frown like that. You look positively fierce."

"Mostly wildly erotic thoughts about you. All X-rated, of course."

Francie didn't respond to the provocative comment, instead she squirmed restlessly in her seat and said, "I'm done with my dessert, Mark. Maybe it's time that we pay the check and head for home. It's going to be really late by the time we get there. And I've got the family dinner thing to contend with tomorrow, since it's Sunday." She made a face at the prospect.

"I'm still scaring you, huh?"

"Maybe a little," she admitted.

He grinned. "That's good."

MARK'S SUV WAS PARKED in a garage about two blocks away from the restaurant. They walked quickly, hand in hand, in the brisk night air to reach it.

The streets were crowded with people, even though it was way after midnight. Of course, in New York City that was nothing unusual for a Saturday night. It truly was "the city that never sleeps," as old Blue Eyes used to sing.

Once they located the car, Mark turned the key in the Explorer's ignition, but nothing happened. There was a clicking sound, but otherwise dead silence.

"That's odd." He glanced over at Francie, who had a suspicious look on her face, and shrugged. "I'm not sure what's wrong. It worked fine when we got here. I'll get out and check. I've got jumper cables in the rear compartment, if we need them. Be right back."

"All right," Francie said, snuggling deeper into her wool coat and wondering if Mark had somehow set this up in advance, although he didn't seem to be the secretive type. After all, he'd just come right out and told her that he wanted to make love to her, and he hadn't seemed to mind when she'd insisted that they drive home after the play.

Looking angry when he came back a moment later, Mark was plowing agitated fingers through his hair. "The battery's been stolen. We'll have to wait until morning to get it replaced."

"What? But...but that's impossible!"

All of Lisa's warnings came flooding back. S-words loomed dangerously on the horizon: seduction, sensuality, *sex*...

Surrender!!

"Don't worry. I've got a friend who lets me use his apartment when I'm in the city. It's only a block or two away from here. He's out of the country at the moment, and I've got a key. We can spend the night there."

Well, how convenient was that?

And how stupid did he think she was?

Francie shook her head, a determined look on her face. "Mark, I'm sorry, but I don't think that's a very good idea. I mean, this is our first date, and I have no intention of sleeping with you tonight."

He grinned, which took a bit of the wind out of her sails. "That's good, because I'm tired. And this wasn't a planned seduction, if that's what you're thinking. If you want to get out and take a look, you'll see that my battery's been lifted. I won't be able to buy a new one until tomorrow. And that's if we're lucky, because there are not a lot of automotive places open on Sunday in the city."

"Don't you have an automobile club, like AAA, you can call?"

"Afraid not. My membership expired while I was in the Philippines. I haven't gotten around to renewing it."

Well, that sounded like a typical male. Not that she could talk. Her membership to Gold's Gym had expired oh...about five years ago.

"How many bedrooms does your friend's apartment have?" If she had to sleep overnight in New York City, she was determined to sleep alone. Not as much fun, but a whole lot safer.

"Just one, but I can sleep on the sofa. That won't be a problem. I'm not going to do anything you don't want me to do, Francie. And like I said, I'm tired. I doubt I could muster up the energy to make love to you tonight."

She didn't know whether to laugh or to feel insulted. "All right. I guess we don't have much of a choice."

He came around, opened her door, and the cold air hit her right in the face, as did the prospect of being in such close proximity to Mark for the entire remainder of the evening.

Francie then thought of another S-word that fit the occasion—*shit!*

11

MARK'S FRIEND'S APARTMENT was cozy, to say the least. Francie wasn't sure they'd be able to walk around without bumping into each other. The place gave new meaning to the word "compact."

"It's smaller than I remembered," Mark said, an apologetic look on his face. "I think I may have been drunk the last time I was here. Everything looks bigger when you're drunk."

Yeah, she'd had a few boyfriends she could say that about. "Didn't you hear? Size doesn't matter." Which was an absolute crock. That was like saying one scoop of ice cream was as good as two, and everyone who ate ice cream knew that was a bald-faced lie.

He grinned, and she smiled, adding, "Just show me where the bedroom is and I'll get out of your way so you can get ready for bed." Just saying "bed" in front of him made Francie feel itchy all over, especially in certain unmentionable places.

"Follow me." He opened the door to what was probably the bedroom. "What the hell!"

"What is it?" Francie tried to see over his shoulder, but couldn't. She surmised from his remark that it didn't bode well for a good night's sleep.

Where was a Ritz-Carlton when you needed one?

"The bedroom has disappeared."

She ducked under his arm and saw what he was talking about. Instead of the usual array of bedroom furniture, there was a mass of expensive-looking photography equipment, not to mention blackout shades at the windows. The photographs on the walls—the ones she could make out, anyway—were downright macabre. Dead body after dead body, and not all of them intact. There was actually one photo of a head with an ax stuck in it.

Toss in a couple of butcher knives and Hannibal Lechter would have felt right at home.

"Is your friend some nut who sleeps on the floor, or something? I mean, it's nice to have a hobby, but isn't this getting a bit carried away? And those photos— Creepy!"

"Steve's a photographer with the A.P., same as me, only he covers mostly homicides. Those are crime scene photos." Rubbing the back of his neck, Mark shook his head and said, "Well, what now?"

"I'll take the couch. You can have the floor," Francie suggested. "How does that sound?"

"Terrible. I'm really tired, and I don't do well on floors."

They walked back into the living room area and found the couch. The edge of a blanket hung out of it, so Francie surmised that it was a sofa bed. "I think your friend sleeps in here." She pulled off the cushions, unfolded the mattress and proved she was right. There was a blanket, but no sheets.

"It looks big enough for two," he said, trying to gauge her reaction.

Optimism was all well and good, but Francie didn't think this was the right time for it.

"I think it might be a queen size," he added hopefully.

"As much as I'd like to accommodate you, Mark, I don't have any nightclothes with me, so I don't think it would be a good idea to share this bed."

And she had no intention of allowing him to see her hairy legs, which she'd neglected to shave, despite her good intentions of this morning.

"Even if I promise to be on my best behavior and find you something to wear? I'm sure Steve has a clean shirt you can substitute for pajamas."

"I don't wear pajamas. I haven't since I entered puberty. I wear a nightgown, usually purchased at Victoria's Secret." In fact, after three *almost* weddings she had more lingerie than she knew what to do with. It figured that the one time she could actually put some of it to use—not that she would, mind you!—it was nowhere to be found.

"As kind as your offer is, I still wouldn't be comfortable parading around in front of you with just a shirt on."

"Tell you what. You can go in the bathroom and change. I'll close my eyes until you're safely under the covers, then I'll hop in. How does that sound?"

It sounded indecently delicious, but she wasn't about to tell him that.

"And what are we going to use for sheets?"

"Be right back." Mark hurried toward the back of the apartment and scrounged up two mismatched sheets—one actually had tigers on it—and a white dress shirt that had obviously just come from the cleaner's—the tag was still fastened to it.

"Here," he said, handing her the hanger. "You go use the bathroom and change, while I make up the bed."

"Are you always this insistent when it comes to your comfort?"

"I've slept on too many bare floors in too many foreign countries to want to do it again. Guess I must be getting old, because the thought of it sends shivers of fear down my spine. I'm really a wuss at heart."

Francie shook her head and smiled, wondering how any woman on the face of the earth could resist Mark Fielding when he grinned the way he was grinning at her now.

Good grief! I'm in trouble.

And there were still her hairy legs to consider!

True to his word, Mark had the sofa bed made upon her return. He was standing next to it, with just his pants on, his shirt tossed casually aside, as though he paraded around half-naked in front of women every day, which was probably closer to the truth than not, she thought, remembering the photographs of all those bare-breasted exotic Polynesian women.

Francie was having a major pectoral moment as she ogled Mark's chest and the rest of his body. "Holy sh—shoot but it's cold in here." His abs were washboard-flat. And there was a nice sprinkling of chest hair. Not too much—she couldn't take the gorilla look—but just enough to be sexy and touchable, sort of like...*her legs?*

"I turned up the heat. It should warm up in here in a few minutes."

Francie thought it was pretty hot already. In fact, she was already in serious meltdown mode. If it got any hotter, she was likely to incinerate right on the spot.

Mark's gaze drifted intently over Francie's body, making her squirm. "You look quite fetching, I must say."

"You aren't supposed to be looking, but since this shirt comes down to my knees, I guess it's okay. What is your friend, a giant or something?"

And who uses the word "fetching" in this day and age? Mark was right out of a Jane Austen novel. Mr. Darcy come to life. And she could be his Miss Elizabeth Bennett, only with a less eloquent vocabulary.

"Steve Slaboda is an ex-football lineman. He played for Syracuse, but a knee injury kept him out of the NFL so he turned to his other love, photography. His heart is as big as the rest of him. He's a great guy and a good friend."

"Steve sounds very nice, and I'm grateful we can make use of his bed, such as it is. Speaking of which— I'm ready to get in, so I'll need you to turn your back until I'm settled under the covers."

"Why? I've already seen everything there is to see. That shirt's transparent in this light, you know."

"What?" Francie's face turned beet-red as she looked down at the stiffly starched white cotton shirt, then back up at Mark, who was grinning from ear to ear like a naughty schoolboy.

"Gotcha!"

Her eyes narrowed. "Watch it, buster, or you're going to end up on the floor. My good humor only extends so far at one o'clock in the morning. Now, close your eyes."

Francie eased onto the bed, glad that the sheets were clean, even if the blankets smelled like Polo aftershave. There were definitely worse smells than Polo—Eddie Bertucci came to mind—so she knew she should be grateful. "Okay, I'm under."

"Close your eyes, unless you're up for a cheap thrill," Mark said.

Francie did as instructed, but she could still see beneath the fringe of her lashes and nearly gasped when he removed his pants. The man looked like a Chippendale dancer, only better. He had on a pair of very brief black underwear and, if the impressive bulge in the front was any indication, he wasn't tired anymore.

She squeezed her eyes shut tighter and tried to swallow around the large grapefruit-size lump in her throat.

"You didn't peek, did you?"

She felt her face warm. "No."

"Liar," he said, and she felt the mattress dip beneath his weight. There was no turning back now.

"I've never slept under tiger sheets before. It's a whole new experience," she said, trying to lighten the awkward moment.

"I've got some black satin ones you should try."

So much for the lighter moment, Francie thought, trying to ignore the fact that her palms were sweating. Wiping them on the shirt, she told Mark, "Just remember to stay on your own side. I like my space when I'm sleeping."

He chuckled. "You sure do have a lot of rules when you go to bed with a man. Are you this way with all your dates, or just me?"

"First of all, I do not go to bed with all my dates! And I think you'll agree that this is an unusual circumstance, so rules are necessary."

"I see." He laughed again.

Francie could feel his body heat and knew she needed to do something to keep her mind off the "other" thing she was thinking about. "Tell me something about yourself that I don't already know."

"Hmm. Well, I come from a pretty normal family, so my childhood was quite happy, for the most part. And I have no homicidal tendencies that I'm aware of, though there have been a few women I could have gladly strangled."

That was reassuring. *Not!*

"Do you have any siblings?"

"Yes, a brother."

"Does he live around here?"

"At the moment he's in Hawaii."

"That's lucky for you. My sister is always under my nose. Lisa would live with me, if I let her, but I won't. We get along better at a distance. I don't need another mother—one is quite enough, thank you very much!—and Lisa tends to smother."

"I like your sister. She's very refreshing, very honest in what she says—a trait you don't find much in women these days."

It was obvious from some of the things he'd said

that Mark had been hurt in the past. Francie wondered who the woman was and if she was still in the picture. The idea that there might be one was depressing and distressing, to say the least.

"Not all women are dishonest, Mark. I try to be truthful in my relationships with men. Well, there have been a few instances where I wasn't totally honest, but I've learned a lot about myself since then, and I'm determined not to repeat past mistakes."

Easier said than done. Because unless she was wrong, Francie was in bed with her next big mistake.

He was quiet for a moment, as if weighing her comment, then said, "Now it's your turn to tell me something about yourself that I don't know."

"Okay, but you have to promise not to tell anyone, or laugh."

He crossed his heart. "Promise."

"I harbor a deep dark secret that is known only to my best friend, Joyce, and my parents. You met Joyce at the party the other night."

"The redhead with the attitude. I remember."

"Yeah, Joyce is pretty hard to forget. Anyway, she and I had this absolutely wonderful idea—at least it was wonderful when we were sixteen—that we would come to New York City and dance with the Rockettes."

"Really? But neither one of you is tall enough, are you? I thought there was some kind of height requirement, or something."

"I don't know. There probably is. When you're sixteen and have your whole life ahead of you, you don't think about things like that. You're naive enough to believe that anything is possible, that you can grow four inches overnight if you need to."

"So why didn't you do it?"

"In a word—Josephine. My mother didn't think becoming a dancer was a suitable profession. She threw such a fit when I first told her, you'd think I had expressed a desire to become a prostitute."

"So you listened to your mother and didn't follow your heart's desire? That's too bad. We only go around this world once and we need to make the most of our dreams."

"As I told you before, my mother is one of my biggest problems. I love her, but trying to please the woman has gotten me into more trouble than it's worth. Not that you could please her, mind you. She's got a huge heart, but a streak of stubbornness a mile long."

"And Joyce? Did she try out for the Rockettes?"

"Actually, she did. But Joyce was never a very good dancer—she has no rhythm—so she didn't make it. I was secretly relieved. Isn't that terrible? I guess I'm not a very good friend."

He reached out and clasped her hand beneath the sheets, accidentally touching her thigh, which made Francie grit her teeth in an effort to keep calm.

"It's normal to feel envy, even if it's about your best friend, and especially when you're sixteen. Don't be so hard on yourself. And you should cut your mother some slack. She loves you and is very proud of you. She told me so."

"Don't be fooled by my mother's Mrs. Brady routine. She's just trying to set you up. She thinks you'd make the perfect husband for me."

He didn't bat an eyelash at her comment. Instead he asked, "How do you know I wouldn't?"

Her eyes widened. "I—I don't. I mean, I'm not in the market for a husband, at the moment, just my mother is. Why? Are you in the market for a wife?"

"I might be. I'm tired of traveling and having no roots. It'd be nice to settle down with someone and maybe have kids someday."

"Do you have anyone in mind?"

He smiled. "Now that's a leading question if ever I heard one." Leaning over, he kissed her lips. "Good night, Francie. Sleep tight."

As soon as his lips touched hers there was instantaneous fire, bells and whistles went off, and Francie knew she wanted more.

A whole lot more.

Sleep was out of the question tonight.

"How tired are you?" she asked, turning on her side and stroking his shoulder in a provocative way that left no question as to what she was asking.

Well, to the normal male, anyway.

"Why?"

Mark wasn't making this any easier, and Francie was not exactly an expert at seduction. She was usually the one being seduced. In spite of her many trips to the altar, she'd never been the aggressive type when it came to men, preferring to let them take the lead.

"Do you want to kiss me again?" she asked, surprising not only Mark but herself.

"Are you coming on to me?"

Well, that was embarrassingly direct.

Was the man dense? Couldn't Mark take a hint? Did she have to spell it out, throw herself on top of him and show him exactly what she wanted?

"Yes. Do you mind?"

He grinned, then reached out to tug her closer to him, surrounding her body with his arms and making her feel small and cherished. "Not at all. I just didn't want to make an assumption that wasn't correct."

She caressed his cheek, thinking that he had to be the most perfect man alive on the planet. "You talk too much. Just kiss me, okay?"

"With pleasure. But I'm going to do a whole lot more than just kiss you, Francie."

Oh, thank heaven! Francie was grateful she wasn't going to have to spell it out for him, after all.

And then she couldn't think at all, because Mark took Francie at her word. His lips were all over her body, making a trail from her mouth, down her neck, to the tips of her breasts, and then into the great beyond where no man had ever gone before, including Captain Kirk of the Starship *Enterprise*.

Oh, she'd had sex before, just not of the oral variety. It seemed her first two fiancés weren't into that sort of thing, even the repulsive Marty, who seemed to be into everything. And she'd never given Matt the opportunity. Though he'd been so reserved, she doubted he'd have done such an erotic thing anyway.

When Mark eased her legs apart and descended, a glorious shiver went straight down her spine to the tips of her toes. She gasped. "Oh...my... That feels so incredible. Don't stop! Please don't stop."

Francie felt like bursting into an operatic chorus of "Sweet Mystery of Life," à la Madeline Kahn in *Young Frankenstein*, but decided she'd better not. Mark may not have seen the classic movie.

She heard him chuckle. "I have no intention of stopping, love. So relax. You are much too tense. Just lie back and enjoy this. I am."

Francie had a bad habit of thinking too much during sex. Usually her mind fantasized, so she could get up a full head of steam toward achieving orgasm. But she wasn't fantasizing now. There was no need. Instead she was contemplating whether or not she should reciprocate.

She'd read in her dog-eared copy of *The Joy of Sex* that most men were wild about fellatio. But she'd never performed it before, and wondered exactly what he might expect.

But she couldn't think about that now, because Mark's mouth was trailing up her stomach again while he positioned himself over her. His penis was probing, even as he sucked her nipples for all they were worth.

Come in! Come in! Francie wanted to shout. *I'm ready for you.*

But he must not have believed that because she felt his fingers enter her. "I want to make sure you're lubricated enough."

"Oh, my!" she heard herself say.

The G-Spot lives!

Pausing for a moment, Mark leaned over the side

of the bed and reached for his pants, withdrawing a condom from the rear pocket—Mr. Ever Ready, apparently—and putting it on. "I'm not hurting you, am I?"

"No! Are you kidding? Not at all." She wrapped her legs around his waist, just in case he thought to change his mind. "Put it in. I'm ready. Put it in. *Now!*"

She thought he was grinning, but couldn't be sure because of the darkness. Then he slipped all seven or eight inches—or maybe it was ten inches, because it sure felt large—into her, and she felt her heart hit the sides of her chest and then explode.

With every stroke she wanted to profess her undying love, to exclaim that he was the best lover she'd ever had—not that she'd had that many, mind you!—and that if he could keep on like this for oh, say, the next hour or so, she'd gladly do his laundry for him tomorrow and maybe for the rest of his life.

"Are you doing okay?" he asked, kissing her lips with great tenderness.

"Yes! Yes! Yes!" she exclaimed with every maddening stroke. "I am doing... Oh! Oh! Oh...!" And then it happened.

All of a sudden lights flashed in front of her eyes, her brain exploded, and she began floating to the ceiling. It was only Mark's body weight that kept her grounded to the mattress.

He achieved his climax, too, in unison with hers, which almost never happened according to the books, and that put the biggest smile on her face, as if she'd just climbed Mount Everest and conquered it.

Just having an orgasm was big. Simultaneous orgasm was gargantuan!

When her breathing finally returned to normal, and Mark had slid off her, she gazed up at the ceiling and said, "Wow! That was fantastic!" She wanted to ask if they could do it again, but then thought better of it.

After all, she didn't want him to think she was greedy.

"Was...was yours okay?" She hated asking that question because one of these days some guy was going to reply, "No. It sucked."

Fortunately, today wasn't that day.

"It was very good, for the first time."

Her eyes widened and she rolled over to look at him, to see if he was joking, but he looked dead serious. "You mean, you've never done this before? Well, I'm impressed. You must be a quick learner."

Mark started laughing and the booming sound filled the entire room for a good thirty seconds. "What I meant to say was that it was good for the first time between us. After we get to know each other better, learn the rhythm of our bodies, we'll do even better."

"No way! I mean, how is that possible? If it got any better I'd have to call the paramedics. See, I have goose bumps on my arms." She held up her arm to show him.

He brushed stray curls away from her face and sighed deeply. "You're something, love, you know that? I had a completely different opinion of you when we first met and now—"

Alarm bells went off. Mark was going to dump her. He hated having sex with her, and he was about to tell her. Even so, she had to know. "And now, what?"

"I'm falling in love with you."

For once in her life, Francie was speechless.

12

I KNOW YOU probably won't believe this, Mark, because I've been doing my best to stay away from you, but I'm in love with you, too.

Mark thought back to Francie's heartfelt admission of the previous night, of the way she had given herself to him completely, no strings attached, no elicited promises of happily ever after, and heaved a sigh, even as he smiled at the memory of their lovemaking.

She loved him.

And he didn't know what the hell to think or to do about it. Or what his feelings were for her.

He'd told Francie last night that he loved her.

But did he?

They'd made love three more times during the night, even though he knew they shouldn't have—under the present circumstances, anyway. But he couldn't seem to help himself.

She had become an addiction. One kiss and he knew he had to have her.

But did he love her?

His feelings were a jumble of confusion. He thought he was so smart, that he had everything worked out, his stupid plan for revenge down to the minutest detail. But now that he'd made love to her—

"Hell, what a goddamn mess!"

And you've got no one to blame but yourself.

The phone rang just then, interrupting his thoughts, which was probably a good thing. Recriminations sucked!

Setting aside his beer, he reached for it, hoping it was Francie—though he didn't know what he'd say to her if it was—and was surprised to find his dad on the other end.

"Hi, Dad! How're you doing? Still working on that tan?"

"Just calling to thank you for that nice little surprise you pulled on your mom and me. It really wasn't necessary. I hate thinking that you spent so much money. But we sure do appreciate it, son. I can't thank you enough."

Mark had called the hotel in Maui where his parents were staying and had paid for an additional two-week vacation for them and his brother. He knew his father would be able to take off the additional time, since he owned his own business, and Matt had already arranged to take off as much time as he needed from his law firm after the fiasco that was his wedding. Mark's motive had been self-serving, of course—he needed the extra time to finish carrying out his plan—and he felt rotten about accepting the gratitude that his father was heaping on him.

"I was happy to do it. It's not often you guys get away, so I figured you should take a little additional time and just relax." That much was true, at least.

He'd missed their last anniversary celebration while on assignment in Turkey, so he didn't begrudge giving them an expensive belated gift. And even though his motives weren't entirely pure, his heart was in the right place.

"Your mom wanted to thank you, too, but she had a hula lesson scheduled for today. That woman's got island fever. I'm not sure I'll ever be able to make Laura leave here. Now she's talking about buying one of those time-shares, so we can spend all of our holidays and vacations over here. She's even mentioned me selling the business and taking early retirement."

Mark grinned at the mental image of Laura in a hula skirt. "Be sure and take lots of pictures, so I can tease Mom when she gets home."

"I will, son. Hold on, your brother just got back from the beach and wants to talk to you. I've got to go find Laura before she runs off with some Hawaiian hunka hunk of burning love."

Mark could hear Matt in the background saying something about jealousy and his dad laughing in response, and he had the sudden urge to fly to Maui and join them.

He wanted to forget all about his plan for revenge, about Francie and all the problems being involved with her had created. He needed to take some time to get his head back on straight. But he knew that wasn't going to happen.

"Hey, bro! How's it hanging?"

Mark thought his brother sounded upbeat. "I take it you've found surfing to your liking?"

"Are you kidding? I love it. And I'm getting pretty

good at the old hang ten," Matt said. "Wish you were here so we could ride the waves together."

"Me, too."

Matt's voice suddenly grew serious. "Listen, Mark, I know Dad's thanked you already for the extension of our vacation, but I wanted to thank you, too. That was really nice of you. And it came at an excellent time."

"You mean, because of what happened between you and Francie?"

There was an uncomfortable silence on the other end before Matt replied, "Not exactly. You see, I've met someone."

Mark's heart did a somersault.

"That's great!" he replied, then remembering his previous advice, toned down his enthusiasm a bit. "I mean, isn't it kind of sudden?"

"That's just it. It isn't sudden at all. Naomi Parker and I went to law school together. She's working here in Maui now. We hooked up when I went to check out some of the law firms I might be interested in joining. We've known each other a long time, but always considered what we had nothing more than just a friendship. But things have a way of heating up over here in the islands.

"Anyway, I'm just glad I have the extra time to pursue this, see if anything develops. I'm thinking that it probably will. At least, I hope so. It feels so right this time. I know I've said that before, Mark, but this time it's the real thing."

"But what about Francie? Are you completely over your feelings for her now?" Mark held his breath, wondering what his brother would say, realizing that it mattered. It mattered very much.

"I think it would have been a huge mistake for me to marry her. Francie's a great girl, don't get me wrong, but we didn't have enough in common to make a life together. I guess you were right—I didn't know her long enough or well enough to make such an important decision. I never even made love to her, if you can believe that. We might have been totally incompatible in the sack."

Mark doubted that very much, but was happy to hear it nonetheless. "Really? That's surprising." He'd just assumed that Francie and his brother had consummated their relationship, and was quite relieved—almost euphoric, if he was honest with himself—to discover they hadn't.

But he didn't want to delve too deeply into why that was so. Not right now, because he needed time to think. Now that the path had been cleared, he had to decide whether or not he was going to go down it.

"Francie always put me off when it came to having sex, and now I can understand why. I guess she sensed that it wasn't right between us. I'm glad one of us had the smarts to know and do something about it before it was too late."

"I'm happy for you, Matt. I hope things work out between you and Naomi."

"You do?" Matt's voice held a note of incredulity. "That doesn't sound like my cautious, relationship-phobic brother. What's changed? Have you met someone?"

Mark took a moment before answering. "Yes, but

it's nothing I want to talk about right now. But when I'm ready, you'll be the first to know." And if that happened, it was one conversation he didn't relish having.

It was one thing to have your fiancée dump you on your ass in front of hundreds of people and quite another to find out that she was now sleeping with your brother. And he just wasn't sure at this point how Matt would react. He didn't want anything, including Francie, to come between him and Matt.

"Sounds mysterious."

"No, just complicated."

Like, where did he go from here?

Did he really want to get involved with someone who couldn't commit?

Been there, done that.

And unfortunately, so had Francie—three times, to be exact.

Did he really want to be fiancé number four?

What if he did decide to pursue her all the way to the altar and at the last minute she bolted? Could his ego ever recover from that? And what of his family? They'd already been put through hell because of what had happened to his brother.

He had plenty of questions, but no answers.

And he was getting way ahead of himself.

Most likely, when Francie found out who he really was, and that his brother was her ex-fiancé, she'd hate him for deceiving her.

And could he really blame her?

"Mark? Are you still there?"

"Yeah, sorry. I was just thinking about something."

"Or someone?" He could hear the teasing laughter in Matt's voice. "Sounds to me like you've been hooked, big brother. Careful you don't relinquish your confirmed bachelor status by losing your heart."

Too late for that, Mark feared, knowing in that very moment that he *was* in love with Francie.

"I'm in love."

Rolling her eyes, Lisa continued to spread peanut butter and strawberry jam onto the four slices of bread for the sandwiches she was making, licking the knife between spreading.

"Oh, please! Not again. I'm telling you, France, you've got to get over this addiction of yours. It isn't healthy. You're becoming a serial bride. Or should I say a serial groom killer?"

"How would you know? You've never been in love, so how do you know it's unhealthy? And I'm not becoming a serial anything."

Lisa paused, knife in hand, which she licked again, then looked up. "It just so happens that I'm in love right now, as we speak, with a great guy. I'm thinking about eloping with him, in fact. But we don't have definite plans as yet."

"What?" Francie's eyes widened as she bolted off the kitchen chair. "When did this happen? Why don't I know anything about it? Does Mom know? Are you crazy?"

"Recently. We met at a dance club. And no, Mom doesn't know, and I want to keep it that way. And I'm not crazy. Actually, for once in my life I think I'm doing the right thing."

"Please tell me he is not another musician. They are so unstable, Lisa. Didn't you learn your lesson the last time, with that crazed trumpet player? My God, the things he threatened to do to you with that mouthpiece."

Sighing at the memory of Tony Jones and his fabulous *horn*, Lisa grinned. "Yeah! That was one incredible night of sex, I can tell you that.

"But you needn't worry, because Alex isn't a musician. In fact, he has a very upstanding job as a mortgage banker. If I marry him, I will become a banker's wife, the image of refinement and respectability. Can you believe that? Mom and Dad would think they'd died and gone to heaven. I can read the headlines now. Screw-Up Daughter Finally Makes Good."

Francie dropped back down in the chair. Her nonconformist, live-life-to-the-fullest little sister was dating a banker? Something was terribly wrong. Lisa was a free spirit who said what she thought and did what she wanted, without giving a whit about convention. She was not the stuff of a staid banker's wife, and Francie worried about Lisa's motives.

Pleasing your parents was one thing, but ruining your life was quite another. Francie was somewhat of an expert when it came to that.

"I don't believe you. You've never dated anyone *normal* in your life. Shall I go down the list?"

Lisa shrugged. "If you like."

"Let's see…there was the female impersonator— the bisexual female impersonator, I might add—the Shakespearean actor with a lisp… And we shouldn't forget the auto mechanic from Brooklyn who called

Mom his love kitten. Major gag." Francie rolled her eyes. "I could go on, but I'll spare you."

Lisa began talking, as if Francie had never spoken. "Alex comes from a very good family."

"Have you met them yet?"

"Well, no. But I know they live in Florida and have oodles and oodles of money. They own a yacht and live on some waterway."

"You can't swim, so the yacht shouldn't impress you that much. And how do you know you'll like them? After all, if you marry the guy, you'll be stuck with his family, too. They could be major snobs."

"Like you considered that before almost jumping into three marriages. And I assume that the new love of your life, about whom you've been talking non-stop, is Mark Fielding, since you've done nothing but brag about how good he is in bed."

"Quit exaggerating, Lisa. I haven't been talking about Mark nonstop." *Have I?* She may have mentioned Mark a time or two—okay, maybe ten or fifteen times, max—but nonstop? Her younger sister was prone to embellishment. And gossip. No doubt Lisa, Leo and Joyce had been discussing Francie's love life without pausing for breath.

"And just what, Miss Hot Pants, do you know about *his* family?"

Sipping her iced tea, Francie paused at Lisa's question, thoughtful for a moment. "Not much, actually. But we haven't known each other very long. I don't want to rush into anything this time, Lisa. I want to be sure before I take the next step, which is why you are not going to tell Mom or Dad about what I've just told you."

Lisa's face fell. "Damn! That's not fair. You know Mom is going to try and get all of the details out of me." She placed the sandwiches on the table and sat next to Francie. "Mom warned me of that when she heard you were going out with Mark. She was so thrilled that she ran down to the church and lit a candle for you."

Suitably horrified, Francie replied, "Nevertheless, you are not to say a word. Promise me. If Mom finds out that I'm interested in Mark she will drag me down to Jacob's Bridal again to buy another wedding dress, and I'm just not ready for that."

"Too bad. She's working on a buy-three-get-one-free deal."

Francie just stared back without saying a word.

"All right. But you can't tell her what I told you about Alex, either. If we decide to get married, it'll be at the spur of the moment. I'm not going to have Josephine Morelli put me through what she's put you through. That would make me totally nuts."

"But if you run off without saying a word, she'll be scared to death. You have to promise to leave Mom a note. It would be cruel not to."

"Oh, all right. I'll send her a telegram from Las Vegas. I'm going to find the tackiest wedding chapel I can and have the wedding performed there. I may even go to that drive-up one that I saw on *Entertainment Tonight*."

"Or the chapel with the Elvis impersonator. That would be a hoot."

Lisa made a face of disgust before taking another bite of her sandwich. "No. Elvis was too much of a pervert. I don't want someone like that performing my ceremony, even if he can sing 'The Hawaiian Wedding Song.'

"I mean, did you see the way he made that poor Priscilla wear her hair? She should have divorced him right on the spot, after she looked at herself in the mirror. I won't even get into the eye makeup. Scary, stuff."

"Dad was right—you have a peculiar way of looking at things."

"And you don't? One day you're marrying Matt Carson and the next you're in bed with some hot guy with major pecs, who you now think you're in love with. How does he feel about you?"

"Mark told me that he thought he was falling in love with me."

"Was that before or after he nailed you?"

Francie grinned and blushed at the same time. "After. It was very romantic, as I recall." And she recalled every exquisite detail.

Who knew she was a screamer?

"Well, sexual compatibility is very important, that's for sure. And from what you've said, you've got no complaints in that department. So maybe it'll work out this time. After all, practice makes perfect. And three times is a lot of practice."

Francie mulled over what she was going to say next, silently debating whether or not she should confide in her sister. After a few moments she blurted, "Have you ever had oral sex, Lisa?"

Lisa's mouth opened and closed, like a floundering fish out of water, and then she replied, somewhat incredulously, "What kind of a question is that? Of course, I have. Why? Are you one of those prudes who doesn't believe in—"

"I just had it for the first time," Francie interrupted, feeling her cheeks redden.

"What?" Her sister's eyes rounded in surprise. "What the hell have you been doing with all those bozos you've been engaged to? I can't believe you were actually going to marry someone who wouldn't give you the big tongue." Lisa shook her head, a look of disgust on her face. "Not good, France. Sometimes I wonder which one of us is really the older sister."

"So I haven't slept around much. Sue me. And you needn't sound so imperious just because you go to bed with every Tom, Dick and Harry that you meet."

Lisa grinned. "So I take it you were pleased with Mark's performance in the cunnilingus area." She flicked her tongue in and out of her mouth rapidly, like a lizard on speed. "Did you do him, too?"

"You are totally disgusting. I don't know why I tell you anything."

"Because your friend Joyce has a bigger mouth than I do. Well, did you?"

"I'm not telling you. It's none of your business." As a matter of fact, Francie had reciprocated and enjoyed the experience very much, but she sure as heck wasn't going into detail with her sister.

And Lisa thought Elvis was a pervert!

Ha! That was rich.

13

"I THINK we should get married!"

Staring at Mark in disbelief, Francie set down the large aluminum pot she'd just filled with water with such force that she nearly dropped it on her foot.

She was making spaghetti and meatballs—her mom's recipe, so she knew it would be good—cooking dinner for Mark for the first time, in the hope of making a good impression. But apparently he was already impressed.

And all she had done was—

Man, she must have been better at *it* than she thought!

They'd spent every waking moment together since the night when they'd made love over a week ago. And when they weren't having lunch, dinner or making love, they were on the phone, talking about everything and nothing.

It was wonderful and very romantic. But still, she had never expected a proposal.

"You're kidding, right? We don't know each other all that well. I mean, I know you said that you were hoping to find a wife someday, but I never thought you meant me." Not that she hadn't been obsessed with the idea, but only in her less rational moments, such as when she was in his arms.

He came up behind her, wrapping his arms around her middle and kissing the nape of her neck, which sent goose bumps up and down her spine. She inhaled the spicy scent of his aftershave and sighed deeply. The man had the power to heat her blood to boiling.

"I've compromised your reputation, so I think we should get married."

She turned in his arms and the first thing she saw was his smile. "Now I know you're kidding." Relief washed through her, as well as disappointment.

"I love you, which is the real reason I think we should get married. I've thought long and hard about this, Francie, and it feels right. We're good together, and you know it. Why wait? Neither one of us is getting any younger."

"As my mother is fond of pointing out," Francie said, shutting off the stove. Taking Mark by the hand, she led him into the empty living room.

Leo, the world's biggest romantic, had graciously bowed out of the apartment this evening when he'd heard who she was entertaining. "Fingers crossed," he'd said with a rakish wink.

Well, it was obvious she didn't need luck in landing Mark. It seemed she had him hook, line and sinker.

If she wanted Mark, and that was a very big *if*.

"Before this conversation goes any further, Mark, there are a few things you should be made aware of."

"What's that?" he said, sitting next to her on the

sofa and reaching for her hand. "I already know everything there is to know about you. You can't scare me off, so don't even try."

She squeezed his hand, wondering if she was being totally stupid and irrational. Mark was a great guy, and she loved him. If she married him, it would solve a lot of problems; mainly, getting her mother off her back. Not that that was a great reason to get married, but it was certainly a viable consideration.

Sanity was too good a commodity to waste!

But her past was something she found difficult to overcome, if she ever could. She loved Mark and would not be unfair to him. "I'm not good at getting married, Mark. I've tried it three different times, with three different grooms, and with the same three disastrous results.

"I've yet to make it stick. I chicken out at the last minute, get cold feet, whatever you want to call it. I'm just not a good marital risk. And I don't think—"

"You think too much, if you ask me. You told me you loved me. Well, I love you, too, and that seems like a good enough reason to get married. And you've already admitted that you weren't in love with those other men you were engaged to. So why not try marrying someone you love? I'm a firm believer in fate, and if fate has sent you to me, then I don't think I can ignore that."

"But you're a romantic, Mark. You're not thinking clearly about this."

"You're wrong, Francie. I've thought a lot about it. I've been dumped in the past, so I'm as leery as the next guy about getting hurt. But I'm willing to take the chance. Remember the Abba song, 'Take A Chance on Me'? Well, that's what I'm doing, only I'm taking a chance on us."

Reaching into his pocket, he brought forth a small blue-velvet box and handed it to her. "I'm thinking with my heart, not my head, and you should be, too. Will you marry me, Francie?"

Francie's hands were shaking as she forced open the lid and stared at a large, round, brilliant cut diamond set in a gold band. "It's beautiful." But she'd had lovely engagement rings before. Well, maybe not this lovely and large, but lovely nonetheless.

"Marry me."

She snapped the case shut, blocking out his plea and the significance of what the ring meant, and handed it back to him, hoping she was doing the right thing. "I need more time to think about your proposal. I'm honored you want to marry me, and I do love you, that's true. But I can't give you an answer right now. It wouldn't be fair to either one of us. I refuse to make another commitment and run away like a frightened child again. I promised myself that I wouldn't. And if I can't keep a promise to myself, then how can I keep one to you?"

"I understand, and I'm willing to give you some time."

Her eyes widened. "You do? You will?"

He nodded. "There are things I need to explain to you, as well, Francie, but I won't get into them right now. When you're sure of what you want to do, and if you say yes to my proposal, then we'll discuss them. I want to be honest about everything that concerns us."

"Do you have a sordid past that you haven't told me about?"

He smiled softly, caressing her cheek. "Not exactly, but there are things, important matters, that we need to get out in the open."

Francie was consumed with curiosity, but she wouldn't press Mark for answers now. That would hardly be fair, since he was allowing her time to make a decision.

"Even though I'm letting you off the hook for now," Mark said, as if reading her mind, "that doesn't mean I'm not going to pull out all the stops to get you to change your mind. I want you to know that."

Thinking that what he'd said was terribly sweet, and very committed, Francie smiled, asking, "What kind of stops?"

"You'll see. It wouldn't be good to reveal my strategy. I'd rather take you by surprise."

Wrapping her arms around his neck, she kissed him passionately. "I like the sound of that. It conjures up all sorts of sexual fantasies. Oh, dear," she said, gazing down at his lap with a wicked smile, "I see you have some, too."

He smiled back with intensity in his eyes that she hadn't seen before. "Paybacks will be hell, Ms. Morelli. I promise you that."

"I'm ready and waiting, Mr. Fielding."

BUT FRANCIE HAD NO IDEA of what she was letting herself in for, and she wasn't prepared for the onslaught that began early the following morning with a visit from her mother.

"I just heard the wonderful news and I had to come right over," Josephine said as she came barreling through the front door, eyeing her daughter, who was still garbed in her robe and slippers. Which made sense, when you considered it was still seven in the morning and Francie didn't have to be at work for two more hours.

"Why didn't you tell me that Mark had proposed, you naughty girl? When do you want to go to the bridal store and pick out your wedding dress? They're going to give me a wonderful discount because I've bought so many there. Mrs. Jacob told me I was one of their best customers."

It was a wonder Mrs. Jacob wasn't giving her mother the entire store, or at least the dress for free. And it wouldn't have hurt the woman to toss in a few bridesmaid's dresses, as well. After all, Josephine had purchased three wedding gowns from the storeowner. It was the least Mrs. Jacob could do to show her appreciation.

Josephine clutched her daughter's face between her hands and squeezed, then kissed her on the lips. "You've made me so happy, Francesca. A mother's prayer has been answered." She crossed herself, giving thanks to the Almighty, who she was sure was in her corner this time.

Francie felt sick to her stomach. "Ma, wait! You're getting ahead of yourself. Who, may I ask, have you been talking to?" As if she didn't know.

I'd rather take you by surprise. Well, Mark sure as hell had. Josephine was quite a surprise at seven o'clock in the morning, or any time of day, really.

Her mother beamed. "Why, my future son-in-law, Mark, of course. Who else? That wonderful boy called me this morning to tell me that he had proposed and that you wanted some more time to decide. So I came over to help you make the right decision.

"Of course, there is only one decision you can make, Francie. You will marry him. Mark is a wonderful man, a piece of bread. You don't find many like him, and such a hard worker. And your children!" She kissed her fingertips. "¡Bellisimo! They will be so beautiful. At last I will have grandchildren. I am so very happy."

Francie headed for the kitchen and the coffeepot, her mother close on her heels. She filled two ceramic mugs, handing one to her mother, who promptly doctored hers with cream and sugar.

"It's too risky," Francie said. "I don't think I can do it. What if I mess up again? What if I can't get through the ceremony, like the last three times? I don't think I could live with myself, if that happened. This time it's different. I love Mark. I couldn't bear to disappoint or hurt him."

"Mark loves you, too, Francie. He told me so. And I already know you love him. I can see it in your eyes whenever you speak about him. What else do you need? It's what was missing those other times. I shouldn't have pushed you so hard before into making a decision. I can see now it was a mistake. But I thought I was doing the right thing, that you were just being stubborn."

"But you're doing that very same thing now, Ma. Don't you see? I'm not ready to make a decision about something so important that will affect the rest of my life. I need more time. Mark understands that. And you need to understand it, too."

Her mother dismissed her words with a wave of her hand. "Sure, sure. Take some time. By tomorrow you will have it all sorted out. I prayed for you, Francie, and so has Father Scaletti."

Of that, Francie had no doubt. The priest announced last week that they were putting a new roof on the church, and she was fairly positive that the Morellis were the ones who had paid for it, three times over. Soon they would be changing the name of the church from St. Mary's to St. Josephine's, in honor of her mother.

Still beaming, as if Francie hadn't spoken a word, Josephine stood and walked to the door. "I've got to go now. I'm meeting with four caterers this afternoon. One is a little more expensive than we wanted to pay, but so what? A wedding isn't the time to be cheap. I explained that to your father.

"And tomorrow there's the florist. And I need to order the invitations. So much to be done, and we still need to set a date. Mark said it was up to you. I'll call you later. Maybe you'll know something by then." With that, she was gone, leaving Francie with a throbbing headache and murderous thoughts.

Mark was going to be killed, that was her first order of business right after she got dressed and went to work.

TED HAD BEEN LEAVING frantic messages on her voice mail for the past two days, wondering why she had been working at home so much, and on the Fielding account exclusively, neglecting her other duties. He needed to talk to her, he'd said.

Francie hadn't had the courage to tell her boss that she'd been working *under* Mr. Fielding, so to speak, not *on* his account. So she wasn't looking forward to this morning's encounter, which would probably be grim.

When she entered her office, it was to find her desktop littered with messages and paperwork that the receptionist hadn't bothered to take care of, as she'd previously been instructed. The incompetent woman would have never considered calling back the clients and trying to work out the problems, or to let Ted handle them. That would have been too much to ask of Gloria Sanchez.

With coffee in hand, Francie sucked in her breath, trying to fortify herself before bearding the lion in his den. "Good morning, Ted." She smiled sweetly at him—though it took some effort—and received a scowl in return.

"Well, well, you really do exist," he said with no small amount of sarcasm as he leaned back in his chair. "I was beginning to wonder if you'd fallen off the face of the earth, Francesca."

"I've been working on the Fielding account."

"Doing what, may I ask? His book isn't even published yet. There can't be that much to do."

"Since Mr. Fielding paid his money so promptly—" *and saved your ass* "—I thought it would be only fair that we begin work immediately on his campaign. I've been busy getting to know the author's background, familiarizing myself with his photography, that sort of thing. I want to do a really good job on this one, Ted."

His look was incredulous. "And for this you missed several days of work? There must have been quite a few photographs to look at."

"I've been working, but at home. I believe I told you that via e-mail and on several voice mail messages that I left on your cell and here. It's not like I've been having fun," she lied, crossing her fingers behind her back.

"You seem scattered lately, Francesca. Are you sure that nothing is the matter? It's not like you to miss so much work."

She sighed, wondering if the man was purposely dense, but knowing he was just plain annoying. "Everything's fine, except for a few family and personal problems."

My mother's driving me nuts!
Our client, Mark Fielding has proposed marriage!
My sister is threatening to elope!
Just business as usual, she wanted to say.

Ted steepled fingers in front of his face and looked pensive for a moment. "I hate to add to your burdens, Francesca, but I'm afraid I'm going to have to let you go."

Francie's mouth fell open, and then she got angry. "But why? I've told you, Ted, I've been working hard. I haven't even used up all of my sick time or vacation days, so letting me go because of a few missed days is just not fair."

"It's not what you think, Francesca. The IRS is shutting me down. I have no choice but to let everyone go."

"Damn!"

"Exactly."

"But what about our clients' deposits? Weren't you able to pay the IRS with that money? I thought you wanted Mr. Fielding's money to square things with them."

Ted hung his head. "I've spent that money and more. I'm not sure how I'll make restitution. At this point, I just can't worry about it. It's likely I'll be filing for Chapter Eleven protection. My lawyer is handling things from here on out."

"Not worry?" *Was he insane or just stupid?* "But I told those people they would be getting individualized service for their money. They trusted me. Now what am I supposed to tell them?" She was thinking about Mark, of course. He had paid a large deposit at her urging, and now he was in jeopardy of losing it all.

"I know you're disappointed, Francesca, but it's difficult being in business in this economic climate. I tried to stay afloat, but it's just not possible."

Francie bit her tongue, knowing it would do little good to lash out at Ted now, to tell him how stupid and dishonest he'd been for years, with other people's money. "I suppose our paychecks are nonexistent, too."

"I'm afraid so." He pulled his wallet from his coat pocket and handed her five hundred dollars, as if that measly amount would make up for all the time and energy she had put into his business. "This is all I can afford to give you. I'm sorry. I know you've worked hard, but I'm no longer calling the shots."

Francie took the money without saying a word, turned on her heel and walked out, shutting the door behind her. She glanced into the outer office, where Gloria, who'd apparently been given the boot, too, was cleaning off her desk. Francie knew she needed to do the same.

"What now?" she asked herself, doing her best not to give in to the tears that threatened. Ted was definitely not worth crying over, that was for damn sure.

The phone rang just then, and it was Leo.

"Hi, sweetie! Just called to see if we were still on for lunch."

"Lunch?" With all that had happened she'd completely forgotten about her date with Leo. "I just lost my job, Leo," Francie told him.

"Congratulations! That job sucked anyway. We'll celebrate down at Pasquale's. No one can feel blue while eating Joe's *calamari fritti*. I'll meet you at noon, okay?"

Francie sniffed, feeling blessed that she had such a wonderful friend. "I love you, Leo."

"I know that, sweetie. And don't worry about finding another job. I've got an idea that I want to discuss with you."

"Okay. I'll see you later."

After she hung up, Francie stared at the receiver and shook her head, wondering what Leo was up to now. And did she really want to know? When her roommate sounded enthusiastic about something, it was usually time to worry.

And what on earth was she going to do about Mark's proposal?

"When my life sucks, it really sucks big-time," she said, tossing most of her stuff in a plastic wastebasket and leaving her old world behind.

LEO WAS SCRIBBLING on the white tablecloth when she arrived at Pasquale's, looking intent and businesslike, which was totally unlike Leo, who shared Lisa's philosophy of live for today.

"Hey, sweetie! Sit down. I've ordered champagne, so we can celebrate your firing in style."

Francie set aside her purse. "I wasn't exactly fired." She explained Ted's situation, and Leo's expression turned grim.

"I hope the Feds burn that bastard. I never did like him. And I didn't understand why you continued to waste your talents on that lousy firm of his."

"But I loved my job. It was challenging, interesting, and I was getting pretty good at it."

"Impossible. No one could love working for and with Ted Baxter. The man makes my skin crawl, and it takes a lot to do that, as you know."

Nodding, Francie finally smiled. "So what did you want to talk to me about? You sounded excited on the phone. Did you win the lottery or something?"

"I've decided to start my own interior design business."

"You're kidding! That's wonderful, Leo." Francie reached out and squeezed his hand, her eyes shining with excitement and happiness for her friend. "But what made you suddenly decide to go into business for yourself? You've never mentioned a thing about it before."

"It was something Mark said when I first met him."

"Mark?"

"He liked my ideas for decorating his apartment and asked me if I was a decorator. I guess the thought took hold, because I've been thinking about doing this ever since."

"Well, you are definitely talented enough."

"Yes, that's true. And I'm a pretty fair artist when it comes to sketching."

"And modesty has never been a problem."

He winked. "Hey, if you've got it, flaunt it, I always say. Anyway, I think you would be perfect as my associate. I'm going to need help getting the business off the ground, and I want you to work with me. Eventually, if things go as well as I think they will, I'll make you a full partner."

If Leo had come right out and told her he'd gone straight, Francie wouldn't have been more surprised. "But I don't know anything about interior design, Leo. And I'm not particularly good at it. You've said yourself that my taste sucks."

"Oh, pooh. I was just kidding. You've got tons of experience working with clients, and that's important. And you've been designing publicity campaigns for years. It's just a different medium. And something you can learn in no time."

"Do you think so?" She shook her head. "What am I saying? I don't know if I want to become an interior designer, and our working together could ruin a perfectly good friendship."

"Why? I'd be a much better boss than Ted Baxter, and I wouldn't try to pinch your ass or touch your breasts, not that they're not great."

"Even if I wanted to accept, I've already had another offer that I'm considering."

Leo's face fell. "Don't consider it. I'll double whatever it is they're going to pay."

"The job wouldn't pay a salary."

"Pro bono work?" he asked, his forehead wrinkling in confusion.

She shook her head. "Mark has asked me to marry him."

"Whoa! I was definitely not expecting that. I hope you said no."

"I haven't said anything, except that I'd think about it. And I'm surprised by your reaction. I thought you were pushing Mark my way. At least, that's the impression I got."

"Oh, don't get me wrong, sweetie. I think you two are perfect for each other. It's nothing against Mark, not at all. I just want you to go slower this time. You've made that walk up the carpeted aisle three times. The runner has to be getting threadbare by now. And I'm running out of places to send you. But if Mark is what you want, if you love him, then you should marry him. And since Joyce is bowing out as your bridesmaid, I'll take her place."

It wasn't difficult to picture Leo in pink satin and lace.

"But what about your job offer? I thought you wanted me to come work for you."

"So what? You can't do both? Since when does marriage mean you can't have a career? Mark would be the first to agree. He's not going to ask you to stay home and become a breeder. After all, unless I'm mistaken, he still thinks you have a career in publicity. Am I right?"

"He does. And I'm going to have to break the news to him that he's just lost a hefty deposit, which he isn't likely to recoup. When he hears that, Mark will probably rescind his marriage proposal."

"On the contrary. I think Mark will think that it was money well spent, since it brought him you."

"Good grief!" Francie rolled her eyes. "I'm surrounded by romantics. There must be an epidemic going around. Cupid unleashed in Philadelphia."

Leo laughed. "So what are you going to do about Mark's proposal, and mine?"

"I'm willing to give your offer a try, Leo, to see how well we work together. It's too good an opportunity to pass up. But I'm warning you that I won't let anything come between us. Your friendship is too important to me."

"Wonderful! That decision calls for more champagne." Leo filled Francie's glass, then leaned over and kissed her cheek. "Welcome to Designing Women. I loved that TV show, didn't you?"

"But you're not a woman, Leo. I mean, not really. So the name doesn't quite fit."

"Oh, sweetie, you're splitting hairs again. So it's one decision down and one to go, right?"

Francie sighed. "You'd better order another bottle of bubbly, because I have no idea what I'm going to do about Mark."

14

FRANCIE PAUSED in front of Mark's door, sucked in her breath, which was minty clean because she had gargled with mouthwash before coming over, and knocked three times with a shaky hand.

She dreaded having to tell Mark that his deposit money had just gone down the toilet, along with Baxter Promotions, and that it was extremely unlikely that he was going to get any of it back. But she knew it was her responsibility to let him know, since she'd been the one to pressure him for it in the first place.

Damn you, Ted Baxter, you fornicating weasel!

"Well, this is a nice surprise," Mark said upon opening the door, leaning down to give Francie a mind-melting kiss. "I wasn't expecting you until tonight. We're having lobster tails for dinner. I just picked them up at the fish market." He stepped aside so she could enter.

Francie's feet felt leaden as she walked farther into the room, sort of like a convict on the way to the gallows. "I doubt you'll want to feed me after you hear what I have to tell you."

His right brow arched. "I thought you wanted to take time to think about the proposal, Francie. It's only been a day. Aren't you going to give it some more time?"

"I—"

"And what are you doing home from work so early? I thought you had a meeting with Ted Baxter today."

"I had my meeting with Ted. It didn't go very well. I was canned."

Concerned, Mark stepped forward and put his arms around her, holding Francie close. "I'm sorry, love. Was it because of me? Have we been spending too much time together? I've been worried about that."

She shook her head. "No. That's what I thought at first, too, but it wasn't that. Ted's been shut down by the IRS. He's not paid his back taxes, or any other that I know of, for quite some time. I guess the Feds got tired of waiting for their money.

"I'm afraid that the deposit you gave me for your publicity campaign is gone, Mark. He pilfered the clients' accounts and spent the money on frivolous items such as girlfriends, hair dye." *Viagra!* The man could have drilled holes in the wall.

"Did you know about his tax problems before I signed on?"

Francie's face filled with color and she was unable to look Mark in the eye, fearful of what she would see. Disdain, anger, blame—all of which she deserved. "Yes. But Ted assured me that he would pay off the IRS and put his financial affairs back in order. I had no idea that he would behave so irresponsibly."

"Or criminally."

"Yes, that, too. He's going to file for bankruptcy, so I doubt anyone will get his or her money back, except the government. I'm so very sorry that I got you into this mess. I hope it wasn't your life savings that you entrusted with Baxter."

"You didn't get me into this, Francie. I came into your office to see you, remember? I was the one who sought your firm out."

"I know. But if I hadn't pushed you so hard to sign with us and insisted on that large deposit—" She felt totally guilty about allowing Ted to manipulate her into doing that. She should have known better. She did know better. She'd just been too spineless to do anything about it.

Clasping the back of her neck gently, Mark guided Francie to the sofa. "You can't shoulder the burden for this crook, Francie. It's Ted Baxter's business that failed, not yours. You just worked there. And from the sounds of it, you're getting the shaft, as well. I doubt you'll get what's due you as far as salary earned, right?"

"Ted magnanimously gave me five hundred dollars, which I'm happy to hand over to you, to make up for what's happened. I know it isn't much but—"

"I don't want your money. But there is another way to make up for what's happened, if you're game." He kissed her cheek with such tenderness that Francie wanted to cry.

"I'm not really sure I'd be a very good bed partner right now, Mark. I feel depressed and—"

"I wasn't talking about having sex with you, Francie. I was talking about love, about the two of us getting married, about you accepting my marriage proposal."

Her eyes widened. "You want me to marry you to make up for the money you lost?"

Well, that was original. She'd give him that.

"Like I told you once before—I'll take you any way I can get you. You already know that I love you, so I don't see the problem."

Gazing into Mark's eyes, Francie saw sincerity and love and knew he had won. She just didn't have the strength to fight Mark, her mother or anyone else right now.

"All right. I'll marry you. But you should know that Leo's offered me a position in his new interior design firm, Designing Women, and I've accepted."

"Designing Women?" Mark arched a brow.

"Don't ask."

"That's great! I know you'll be good at it."

"And don't say I didn't warn you about what could happen on our wedding day. There are no guarantees that this time will be any different than the last three. I might not be able to make it all the way to the altar."

"Oh, but you're wrong, Francie. There's a huge difference. You love me, I love you, and I don't intend to let you get away this time, with anything."

She was a bit taken aback by his vehemence. "That sounds like a threat, not a proposal."

"It is, in a way. I'm determined that you will be at the church on the appointed day and time, suitably dressed in your wedding finery, and ready to say your 'I dos.' I may have to hogtie and drag you in front of the priest myself, but you are definitely going to be there."

Francie's hand went to her pounding heart. She felt as if she was reading one of those romance novels where the hero takes the heroine and ravishes her— *quite thoroughly, I might add!*—then drags her by the hair to the altar, insisting that she marry him or face the consequences of his pulsing desire.

Okay, so she'd read a lot of romance novels.

"Well, you certainly sound determined. If I didn't know better, I'd say you had some deep, dark, ulterior motive for wanting to marry me."

Mark got a peculiar look on his face, then, after a moment, he smiled. "I can assure you that my motive has been the same from the beginning. Nothing's changed, except that I love you more today than I did yesterday."

"Remember what I said a while ago about not being in the mood to make love?"

"Yes."

"I lied."

"THAT SHADE OF GREEN makes my skin look sallow. It's ghastly, so plebian. I don't like it. I think we should look for something else, Francie. Something with a little more pizzazz."

Francie shot Leo a look of pure unadulterated disgust, ignored Lisa's widening grin, and asked the salesclerk at Jacob's Bridal—a stout, unfriendly woman in her sixties, who had more facial hair than Leo—to show them a few more bridesmaid dresses.

Leo, despite his *generous* offer to wear a dress,

would be garbed in a tuxedo, made out of the same color the other bridesmaids were wearing, as befitted his position as Francie's maid of honor.

Since Joyce had bowed out, due to financial concerns, and her sister didn't want the position, because of the impending flight possibility, Francie had no choice but to accept her roommate's offer. A decision that did not sit well with her mother.

"Who has a man for a maid of honor?" Josephine had wanted to know when Francie first informed her. "We will be laughed out of the church, not to mention excommunicated when Father Scaletti finds out that Leo is...different."

"If I can't have Leo, then I won't get married," was Francie's firm response. Her mother's acquiescence was immediate, though not without additional comment.

Josephine was a master at having the last word.

"What's wrong with green? I like green," Francie's mother asked, scowling deeply. "Many bridesmaids wear green. Rosa Bartolomo's daughter had green dresses at her wedding, and she's given Rosa three grandchildren already. Besides, I look good in green, everyone says so."

Leo shook his head. "No, you don't, Mrs. Morelli. You have very olive skin and green makes you look washed out."

Horrified that what Leo said could possibly be true, Josephine rushed to the closest mirror. Now that the man was passing himself off as an interior designer, she gave his opinion a teensy bit more respect.

Francie sighed. "You've already objected to pink, yellow, turquoise and now green, Leo. What's left?"

He grinned. "Well, I was thinking that a deep red would be nice, maybe a cranberry. Not everyone uses it, and it would really make a statement."

"Red!" Francie's mother turned back and crossed herself, then shook her finger at Leo. "Are you nuts? What kind of suggestion is that? Red is not a color for a wedding, or a bridesmaid. It's indecent."

"I like the idea," Lisa piped in. "Those pukey pastels make me gag. And with your coloring, France, I think red would be stunning, a nice compliment to your cream dress."

The wedding dress she'd finally chosen was ivory satin, not cream, but Francie wasn't going to go there now.

Actually, where she wanted to go was home. Take a nice hot bath and maybe drown herself in two dozen chocolates and a bottle of wine.

They'd been at this wedding planning thing since the night she'd accepted Mark's proposal. It was a familiar path and one Francie had hoped never to tread again.

First, there was the torturous ordeal of selecting her wedding gown. Everyone, except Mark, who hadn't been allowed to accompany them because of the superstition thing, had offered an opinion on what she should wear.

It had to be original, and totally different from the last three—no easy feat!—so it wouldn't bring bad luck to the proceedings, as her mother had patiently explained to anyone within earshot.

Next had come the selection of the caterer. She'd finally decided on Manny's Little Italy Deli, much to her mother's disgust and disappointment. But Manny was a friend, had been involved, so to speak, in the other three wedding escapes, and would do a wonderful job with the food. The reception was to be held in the fellowship hall of the church, and Manny had promised to handle all of the details, which would be a big load off of her.

"Maybe Mark and I should just elope." Francie spoke her thought out loud without even realizing it. Lisa's head shot up, an alarmed look on her face.

What are you doing? she mouthed silently.

Francie smiled apologetically and shrugged.

"Elope! *Madre de Dios!* What are you talking about? I would be brokenhearted if you did that, Francie. You know that. Don't talk such nonsense. We'll find the right color. There's no need to get upset.

"Isn't that right, Lisa?" Josephine asked her other daughter.

Lisa, who was staring daggers at her sister, nodded. "Right. We're all looking forward to you and Mark having a big wedding. It's so much nicer than having a big mouth, don't you think?"

Josephine shrugged in confusion. "What does she mean, Francie?"

Lisa forced a smile. "Nothing, Mom. It's a private joke between me and Francie."

"This is all such a bother and I don't believe for a minute that anyone, with the exception of Mom, is enjoying themselves," the bride-to-be said. "I know I'm not."

"You know what we all need right now?" Leo suggested, jumping up from his seat, his face wreathed in a huge smile.

"A psychiatrist?" Francie supplied.

"No, a trip to La Taverna. We will drink ouzo, eat stuffed grape leaves and baklava, and watch the belly dancer. No one can stay in a bad mood after doing that."

Josephine looked at Leo as if he'd lost his mind. Then she asked as much. "Has your friend lost his mind, Francie? I am not going to watch a belly dancer. It's indecent."

"Oh, lighten up, Josephine," Leo told Francie's mother, who gasped in shock. "Your daughter needs a break from all this wedding stuff. We all do, including you. And it'll be fun."

"But...what about my husband? I need to go home and fix John dinner."

"Your husband can order a pizza tonight. He's a grown man. He'll get along fine without you. Besides," Leo added wisely as an afterthought, "don't you want to be included in Francie's bachelorette party? All the females in the wedding party are supposed to be there."

For someone who liked to have her finger on the pulse of everything, Leo had made the one suggestion that was sure to tempt Francie's mother, and everyone knew it. "I guess it's my duty as mother of the bride to go and chaperone." She looked uncertain but determined to do what was expected of her.

"Exactly." Leo turned to Francie's sister. "Lisa, go

out front and flag down a taxi," he ordered. "This shindig is on me."

"But what about the bridesmaid dresses?" Josephine wanted to know, staring at the salesclerk, who looked just as confused as she did.

"Order two bridesmaid gowns in deep red, and the one tuxedo. You have the sizes and measurements on file. If we need to come in and have fittings later on, we will."

Francie had made a quick decision and felt empowered. She needed to hang around Leo more often. The man was nothing short of a genius.

MARK'S PARENTS had just called. They were back from vacation. And now the shit was going to hit the fan, because Mark had the depressing chore of telling them and his brother just what he'd been up to these past few weeks.

By the way, I'm getting married, to Matt's ex-fiancée, Francesca Morelli.

Yeah, that should go over really well.

Before he could change his mind, Mark pulled his SUV out of the parking garage and headed in the direction of the Fairmount Park area, where his parents lived.

It was not going to take that long to get there, even though he was traveling at only twenty-five miles per hour to give himself more time to get his story straight.

He still hadn't told Francie what he'd done, who his brother was or why he'd decided to perpetrate such a ruse. Mark had no idea how she would react, though he knew it wasn't going to be pleasant.

The hell of it was, now that he knew he loved her, he didn't want to risk losing her.

Mark was going to go through with the wedding. He'd finally decided that, though he hadn't been one hundred percent certain until the day she'd lost her job.

Making love to Francie that day, while she was hurt and vulnerable, had cemented his feelings. If he'd had any doubts before, that day had erased them.

"Mark, we weren't expecting you so soon," his mother said when he arrived on her doorstep. "Dad's out in the backyard watering the plants, which are half dead, unfortunately. And Matt's on the phone with Naomi. I assume he's told you about the new love of his life."

Kissing Laura on the cheek, Mark followed her into the kitchen and accepted the iced tea she set in front of him.

"Now, tell me all about what you've been doing while we were gone. Your father said you hadn't been working much these past couple of weeks, just dabbling at home, for the most part. I'm glad you took some time off. I've worried that you've been working too hard."

"You shouldn't worry about me, Mom. I'm fine. And it might be better to wait until everyone comes in, so I don't have to explain things twice. What I have to tell you is going to come as quite a shock, I'm afraid."

Laura clutched her throat. "You've been fired?"

"Who's been fired?" Steve Fielding asked, entering the kitchen through the back door after wiping his muddy boots on the wooden mat first. "Hey, son. Good to see you. What's this about being fired?"

"No one's been fired." Mark noticed how tanned and healthy his parents looked. "You've got quite a tan, Dad. Looks like you and Mom have turned into a couple of beach bunnies." There was a romantic light in his parents' eyes, so he knew they had enjoyed their island interlude, which made him happy.

Matt came in just then and sat at the table. "I was on the phone," he explained after greeting Mark with a hug. "I missed you, big guy."

"Sounds like you didn't have time to miss me."

"Things are great between Naomi and me. We're already talking about setting a date for a wedding."

"Oh, Matt, isn't it kind of sudden? After all, you haven't dated Naomi very long. I don't want you getting hurt again."

"I'm fine, Mom. I'm completely over Francie."

"So if she married some other guy, you wouldn't care?" Mark asked.

Matt shook his head. "No! That's over and done with. I explained that, remember?"

"I just wanted to make sure."

"Why, son?" Steve asked his eldest. "What's it to you?"

Mark loved his father, but the man had a mighty uncomfortable way of cutting right to the chase. "I know this is going to come as a shock to all of you, and I fully intend to explain the details of how I got here, but I'm going to be getting married in a few weeks."

"But that's wonderful!" Laura exclaimed, rising out of her chair.

"To Francesca Morelli."

There was dead silence. Laura dropped back down in her seat. Steve's eyes widened, even as his jaw dropped. And Matt, who Mark had expected to punch him in the nose, burst out laughing.

"You're kidding! You and Francie?"

"It didn't start out in the way you'd expect." Mark went on to explain his indignation at the way Francie had treated Matt on their wedding day, and his subsequent plan to take his revenge on her.

"So you're marrying this woman out of spite?" his father wanted to know, shaking his head, his eyes filled with concern. "I don't like that, son."

"No, not anymore. That was the original idea, but I fell in love with her. Don't ask me how."

"And Francie is fine with this?" Matt asked. "I find that hard to believe."

"Francie doesn't know anything about why I sought her out. I passed myself off as a potential client for her company."

"Oh, Mark, you didn't?" Laura reached out and clasped her son's hand, worry and sadness filling her eyes. "Francie is going to be devastated when she finds out. You must tell her, give her the chance to decide whether or not marrying you is truly what she wants. You can't marry that girl and then tell her after the fact. That wouldn't be fair."

"Why not? I was thinking that we'd just get married, and then, in about five or ten years, I can tell Francie the truth." Mark had it all figured out, or so he thought.

"You really love this woman, don't you?" his father asked.

Mark clasped his head in his hands. "More than anything. And I've messed it all up."

Matt grinned. "Well, they say God works in mysterious ways, and I guess this is your punishment for being a lying, conniving bastard, bro."

"Matt, such language!" Laura chastised.

"I learned it from Dad."

Steve shot his son a deadly look. Matt grinned in return. "That's not true, dear. The boy is just trying to cover his butt."

Laura pushed herself up from the table, said, "There are times when I wish I'd had daughters," then walked out of the kitchen, a disappointed look on her face that filled Mark with sadness and disgust, at himself.

"Mom's pissed. I've never seen her like that," Matt said, patting his brother's shoulder. "You have my blessing, Mark, if that's any help."

"Thanks. It is."

"I'm not sure how you're going to fix this mess, son, but I know you'll do the right thing. Your mother is right—you can't have a marriage that's been perpetrated on a lie."

That night, alone in his apartment, Mark thought about what his parents had said, and knew they were right. He had to tell Francie the truth and suffer the consequences.

And probably a few broken bones.

At least he'd be spared confessing his sins tonight. Francie had gone to an all girls' party. With Leo.

Go figure!

Tomorrow would be soon enough to tell all. He just wasn't sure how the hell he was going to do that, and what he was going to say.

15

MARK HAD SPENT the past few weeks waiting for just the right moment to tell Francie about his deception.

Not that there would ever be a good time to tell her.

And not that he'd found that perfect moment yet.

Their respective schedules had not been conducive to private discussions of such an important nature, which had added to the problem—and his limitless list of excuses.

Francie had been busy assisting Leo with plans for the new interior design business, looking for just the right location to set up shop, picking out suppliers, arranging for advertising and the dozens of other things involved with beginning a new enterprise. Mark had been sent on assignment to Oregon for almost a week to cover a major oil spill. And they'd both been consumed with dining invitations from various members of the extended Morelli family who wanted to get better acquainted with Mark.

Which had brought up the inevitable question from Francie, "When am I going to meet your family?"

The time had come. There was no putting it off any longer, and Mark knew it.

In fifteen minutes he was due over at Francie's

apartment for dinner, and to help pick out the menu for their wedding reception, which was just a few short weeks away.

Mark had never considered himself a coward. But he felt real fear now.

His future happiness rested in Francie's hands. He couldn't imagine a life without her in it and he had to convince her not to break their engagement.

Hell, he had to convince her not to kill him!

ALL DAY, Francie had been looking forward to having dinner with Mark and then afterward maybe some deliciously sinful *dessert*. They'd hardly spent any time alone in the past few weeks, and she missed that. And him.

In just a short time he'd become as necessary as air to her. She'd fallen hard this time and could finally admit to herself, without any doubts, recriminations or misconceptions, that she was hopelessly in love.

Mark was the one she'd been waiting for all her life. The others had been placeholders, stand-ins, while she'd waited for the one true love of her life to show up.

"Mrs. Mark Fielding. Francesca Fielding." She liked the sound of that, she thought, smiling happily.

When the knock sounded at the door, Francie got a strange fluttering in her stomach. "It must be true love," she said, feeling happier in that moment than she'd ever felt before.

Licking the chocolate frosting off her fingers, Francie untied her apron. She'd gone all out tonight with the dinner she'd prepared for Mark, hoping to show off her domestic side—roasted leg of lamb, new potatoes in butter with parsley, and the most decadent chocolate cake ever created by human hands.

Chocolate, sex and Mark were definitely a dynamite combination!

Opening the door, she found the object of her erotic thoughts standing there, but he didn't look at all happy to see her. In fact, Mark looked downright nervous and sick to his stomach, if his ashen complexion was any indication.

"What's wrong? Are you sick? Did something horrible happen?"

Mark handed her a bottle of wine—cabernet sauvignon, her favorite—and shook his head. "No, not yet."

Confused by his cryptic remark, she took his hand and led him into the living room where she had two glasses of champagne and a hot wedge of Brie with crackers waiting. "Help yourself. Dinner's going to be a few minutes. I miscalculated the time on the roast."

"That's just as well. We have to talk."

Francie didn't like the ominous sound of Mark's statement, or the gloomy note to his voice. Was he going to break their engagement? Had he changed his mind about loving her? After all, theirs had been a whirlwind courtship. Regrets were known to happen.

Didn't she know that in spades?

"Tell me what's wrong. Have you changed your mind about getting married? Do you have cold feet?"

"Christ, no!" He shook his head. "Quite the opposite, in fact. I'm just afraid you're going to, after I confess what I've done.''

"You're married, is that it? You have a wife and three small children?'' Though she meant it as a joke, she crossed shaky fingers behind her back, praying it wasn't so.

"No, I'm not married. It's nothing like that. It's something I've done, something I'm not very proud of, and something you're likely to hate me for.''

"You've had an affair with one of your old girl-friends?''

He sighed. "I wish it were that simple.'' Reaching for her hand, he pulled her down next to him on the sofa. "Francie, I've done something terrible. I wouldn't be able to live with myself if I didn't tell you before the wedding. I'm praying you won't change your mind about marrying me. I love you, and I want to spend the rest of my life with you.''

She caressed his cheek. "Why would I change my mind? Nothing can be that awful. I love you. Just tell me what it is and get it over with. I'm sure it's not as bad as you think.''

Mark plowed agitated fingers through his hair. "I haven't been honest with you. I—'' He swallowed. "I don't know how to say this. I'm such an idiot, an ass.''

"Let me be the judge of that, okay? You're starting to scare me.''

"I'm Matt Carson's stepbrother. My parents are Steve and Laura Fielding.''

It took a moment for his words to sink in, and when they did, Francie's brows creased in confusion. "Matt's stepbrother? I don't understand. What am I missing?" But she was getting a very bad, throw-up kind of feeling in the pit of her stomach.

Taking a deep breath, Mark did his best to explain. "I was going to be best man at your and Matt's wedding—the surprise he didn't tell you about. When I got to the reception and found out how distraught my brother was because you'd dumped him, I decided to get revenge."

Francie's face paled. "And that's why you showed up at Baxter Promotions, to get revenge? But how?"

This had to be a sick joke, a nightmare she hadn't yet woken up from.

"My plan was to woo, bed and then almost wed you. I was going to dump you at the altar, just as you had dumped my brother and those other men."

"But why? I mean, I can understand your being upset for Matt, that's understandable. But you didn't know me, didn't know the reasons behind my leaving him or my other fiancés at the altar. How could you judge me without all the facts?"

"I shouldn't have. I know that now. After I got to know you I understood better why you had done it. And even though I was still upset for Matt, I couldn't dislike you anymore. In fact, I grew to love you. My love, my proposal, the fact that I want to marry you, that is all real."

Shoulders stiffening, Francie pulled her hand from his grasp, her eyes narrowing. "How do I know that? How do I know that everything you've told me, every word of love, was not a sham? You seem to be quite good at deception. You sure had me fooled."

"It wasn't...isn't. I swear. I'm in love with you,

Francie. I want you to be my wife. That ring on your finger is proof of that. It was my grandmother's."

She gazed down at the ring, which didn't seem to shine as brightly now, and sighed. "Was Matt a part of this?" She had a hard time believing that he would do such a thing. Matt was too honest and sweet to have been a party to something so heinous.

Mark shook his head. "No. My parents and Matt went to Maui for a vacation. They were out of the picture when I implemented this stupid scheme."

"I see."

He held out his hands beseechingly. "Francie, I'm sorry. Truly, I am. Please forgive me."

"I think you'd better leave, Mark. I'm not thinking clearly right now, and I might say something I'll regret later. Please leave. I have to have time to think, to sort this all out."

To eat fifty gallons of fudge ripple ice cream.

"Don't hate me, Francie. I know what I did was childish and destructive, especially since I didn't know anything about the kind of woman you are. I'd been hurt in the past by unfaithful, unfeeling women and—"

"And you lumped me in with them?"

Bastard!

"I guess I did. But now that I know you, I realize I was wrong, that it couldn't be further from the truth. I love you. Please believe that."

"I don't know what to believe anymore, Mark. I've been planning a wedding, a life with you, thinking seriously about having your children...and it's all been based on lies. I feel used, stupid and very, very angry."

And hurt. So much so that her heart ached with it.

"Not all of it was a lie. My love is the genuine article."

"How do I know that, after everything you've said? I don't really know you at all, do I?"

He rocked back on his heels as if slapped. "Because I'm telling you the truth, that's why. There's never been anyone who has touched my heart and soul the way you have. I surrendered my heart the first time I kissed you and made love to you. I knew then that I could never go through with my asinine plan for revenge."

Francie felt her eyes swelling with tears, but she refused to let Mark see her cry over him. "Please go home, Mark. I need a few days to think about things, see where we go from here."

"I love you, Francie. Please remember that," he said, kissing her cheek. He stood and walked to the door, pausing to look back, his face a mask of pain and regret. "When can I see you again?"

"I don't know. I'll call you."

But she wouldn't. Not for a long time.

Maybe not forever.

FRANCIE HAD BEEN WALKING around in a daze for a week, and she was still no closer to deciding what she was going to do about Mark.

She loved him. That was still a certainty. Despite everything he had done to deceive her, her love for him was as strong as ever, a never-ending entity.

But could she marry him?

Francie wasn't sure.

She'd made so many mistakes in the past. How could she compound those mistakes by making another? It was clear that she sucked in the judgment department.

Knowing that, she'd talked things over with Leo, who had told Francie she'd be crazy to break off her engagement to Mark. He had advised her to marry "the poor bastard and put him out of his misery."

Apparently, Mark had cried on Leo's shoulder a time or two.

Surprise! Surprise!

Men always stuck together.

So it had come as quite a shock to learn that Lisa shared Leo's opinion. Her sister had advised Francie to forgive Mark and proceed with the wedding as planned, saying Francie would regret it for the rest of her life if she made any decision other than to marry Mark.

But when had Lisa ever been right or decisive about anything? One minute she was eloping and the next—

And then there was Joyce. Even her pragmatic best friend, who was not a huge fan of the male species, had advised her to go ahead with the wedding. And Joyce, for all her faults, had never lied to Francie. She told it like it was, painful or not, and Francie had always taken her advice.

But what about now?

Confused, and at wit's end, she decided to seek out the one person who might actually be able to offer some insight into her problem, as farfetched as that seemed.

Francie entered her mother's kitchen and found Josephine alone, standing at the stove, stirring a pot of beef stew. The pungent smell of onions permeated the warm room, making her stomach rumble.

One thing Francie hadn't lost was her appetite. In fact, quite the opposite was true. Anxiety and unhappiness made her eat like there was no tomorrow. She'd been devouring ice cream, chocolate and anything else edible she could get her hands on.

Francie had eaten at such an alarming rate and quantity that Leo had taken to calling her Miss Piggy.

And Leo called himself her friend. Ha!

"Hi, Ma!"

Josephine, who knew nothing of her problems with Mark, turned and smiled widely. "There's my favorite bride-to-be. What are you doing here, Francie?" She glanced at the big round clock on the wall that always reminded Francie of the man in the moon. "I thought you were going for the final fitting of your wedding dress today. Do you want me to come with you? Is that why you've come?"

Her mother seemed so excited at the prospect Francie was reluctant to burst her bubble, but knew she had to. "We need to talk, Mom. I'm thinking about canceling the wedding."

"What?" Wiping her hands on her apron, Josephine rushed forward and took her daughter's hands, concern covering her face. "What happened? You can trust your mother with the truth. Is Mark abusive? Did he hit you? Does he carry on with other women? Because if that's so—"

Heaving a sigh, Francie shook her head. "No, Ma, it's nothing like that."

Crossing herself, Josephine breathed a sigh of relief. "Thank the good Lord! I was frightened for you. There are so many crazy people in this world."

Seating themselves at the old Formica table, Josephine pushed a plate of sugar cookies toward her daughter. "Eat. It will make your problems seem lighter. Now, tell me what's wrong. Why must you cancel your wedding?"

"Mark deceived me."

Josephine gasped. "With another woman? *¡Bastardo!*"

As if by rote, Francie explained for the fourth—and she hoped final—time the story of Mark's revenge against her, including his avowals of love and her feelings of mistrust. "I don't know what to do. I'm sad, confused and very hurt by everything that's happened."

"You have done the right thing by coming to your mother." Josephine patted her daughter's hand consolingly. "Do you still love Mark?"

"Unfortunately, I do. And he says he loves me. But still, that doesn't make up for what he's done, or was planning to do."

After a few moments Josephine nodded. "I agree. You shouldn't marry him. I think it would be best if you break it off, call it quits."

Francie's eyes widened. "What? But that's the last thing I expected you to say." And probably the reason she'd come to get her mother's advice in the first place. Four for four would have been the cincher in helping her to decide whether or not she should go through with the wedding.

"As much as I want you to get married, I don't want you to marry someone you feel you can't trust, or who can't make you happy. You would be miserable for the rest of your life."

"But Mark does make me happy, deliriously so. At least, he did, before all this happened."

"Has he called?"

She nodded. "At least twenty times a day. My answering machine is full of his messages. He's come over, too, but I refuse to see him. Leo's been running interference for me."

"He sent flowers?"

"Dozens of bouquets, all with little cards that say how sorry he is and how much he loves me."

"Jewelry?"

"No."

Josephine made a face. "Well, you can't expect everything, but a diamond and emerald bracelet would have been nice."

"He did send a giant teddy bear." With a red heart hanging around its neck that said, I Love You!

"That is good. It shows he knows he did wrong and is trying to make it right. I will go talk to him."

"You?" Francie's eyes widened, right before her gut clenched. "You're going to talk to Mark? Whatever for?"

"To see where his heart is in this matter. If I feel

that he is being honest and contrite, then we will proceed. If not, we will cancel the wedding."

"But shouldn't that be my decision? I mean, I am a grown woman. I do know my own mind. Well, I used to. Just not right now." Francie heaved a disheartened sigh, wondering why her almost-perfect future had gone down the shitter.

On second thought, a visit from Josephine was just what Mark deserved.

"Exactly. You are too close to the situation and not thinking clearly right now. You need someone objective who can decide what the best thing is to do."

Well, they didn't call her The Terminator for nothing. If anyone could dissect and interrogate Mark Fielding, it was Josephine Morelli.

"Isn't it a bit cowardly of me to let you handle this? The one thing I've fought against all my life is having you push me into making decisions I don't want to make."

"I promise this time I won't push. I'll just find out the facts and tell you what I think. You will make the final decision about the wedding, and your father and I will abide by it."

Jaw unhinging, Francie's asked, "You're kidding, right?"

"The only thing I have ever wanted is your happiness, Francie."

"And grandchildren. Let's be honest."

Josephine smiled. "And grandchildren. But I want your happiness even more than the *bambinos*. I have been very happily married to your father these many years, even though at times it doesn't seem so. I want the same for you, Francesca. I want you to find happiness with someone you can love and respect, and who will love and respect you in return."

Wow! Was this woman sitting here really her mother? Or had the real Josephine Morelli been taken by aliens and replaced with a clone?

After a few moments Francie said, "Okay, Ma. We'll do it your way."

And let the chips fall where they may.

TRUE TO HER WORD, Josephine paid a visit to her daughter's fiancé later that same afternoon. She had four questions for Mark.

"Do you love my daughter?"

"Yes!"

"Are you sorry for what you have done and willing to make penance?"

"Yes!"

"Are your parents willing to chip in on the wedding reception?"

"Of course."

"Are your sperm healthy and strong swimmers?"

"I... I think... Yes."

Satisfied with his answers, Josephine left Mark standing in the middle of the living room with his mouth gaping open, and headed over to her daughter's apartment.

"I had a serious discussion with Mark," she told Francie upon entering. "He says he loves you very much and will do everything in his power to make it up to you. I think travel and expensive jewelry are not out of the realm of possibility."

Remote in hand, Francie clicked off the TV show she'd been watching, a dismayed look on her face. "But, Ma, I don't want expensive gifts. That is not what this is all about."

"Don't be stupid, Francesca! When a man has been wrong about something important he must pay through the nose. It is the way of things. Women of the world must stick together on this matter.

"Anyway, I had a very to-the-point talk with Mark. The man is very distraught about what he has done. After searching my soul and praying to God, I've decided that you should marry him. He loves you, you love him. What could be better?"

Francie's eyes rounded. "You do? But I thought you said—"

Josephine waved away her daughter's objections. "Yes, I am certain it is the right thing. Mark is a good man. And the fact he is a man explains a lot about why he does the things he does. It's the nature of the beast. But you can take him in hand and make him toe the line once you're married. Don't be afraid to..." Josephine's brows rose up and down. "You know."

At her mother's innuendo, Francie gasped. "Ma! That's terrible. Women aren't supposed to use sex as a weapon."

"And why not? We don't have that many weapons to use. God gave us that one, so we should take advantage when we can. It's only fair."

For some strange reason, whenever her mother explained things, it sort of made sense. Why was that?

"Thanks for your help and advice, Ma. I'll take over from here."

"So you're going to marry him, no?"

"Maybe. I haven't decided yet."

But, of course, she had.

Josephine's face filled with pleasure. "That's good enough for me. I'll call Father Scaletti and tell him the wedding is to go on as planned."

"You told Father Scaletti about this? How embarrassing. How am I supposed to face him now?"

"He's my spiritual advisor, Francesca. Of course, I told him. Now be a good girl and go kiss and make up with your fiancé."

Kissing her mother goodbye, Francie headed straight for the refrigerator. She needed sustenance, a lot of it, while she decided what she was going to say to Mark.

16

IT WAS A BAD DAY for a wedding.

Right?

Francie wasn't the least bit sure of anything as she gazed down the red-carpeted aisle—Leo was right about the carpet being threadbare—to where Mark was waiting for her at the altar. Standing next to him was the best man, his brother, Matt.

And how weird was that?

The church was packed. Even Aunt Flo had decided to dress up for the occasion. She looked a little less bag-ladyish than usual. Grandma Abrizzi was wiping tears from her eyes with a pretty lace handkerchief, probably because she'd been seated next to Aunt Flo.

Mark looked extremely handsome in his tux and very confident.

And why shouldn't he be?

Her *almost* husband had hired off-duty police officers to stand at the rear of the church, in front of the doors, just in case Francie changed her mind and decided to run.

She should have been furious with him, especially after everything that he'd done, even though she'd forgiven him.

Make-up sex was really rather fantastic!

But Francie was so stupidly in love with Mark Fielding that instead of being upset, she thought it was the most romantic gesture any man had ever made.

Good grief! She was going to barf.

But not because she was nervous; she wasn't the least bit nervous—okay, maybe just a little bit—but because her thoughts were so sickeningly sweet.

Marrying Mark felt right. She had no doubts about that now. And she had her mother, of all people, to thank.

When Josephine had uttered those prophetic words—*He loves you, you love him. What could be better?*—Francie'd had no argument. She'd known in that moment that she was going to become Mrs. Mark Fielding, for better or worse, in sickness and in health, and in Paris, where they were going on their honeymoon, as soon as the wedding formalities were over and done with.

Paris. Mark. Sex!

She could get used to this marriage thing. Staying single was highly overrated, in her opinion.

Glancing down the aisle at her mother, Francie was surprised to find that the woman was wearing a distraught rather horrified expression.

"What's wrong with Ma?" she whispered to her father, who had her arm clutched so tightly he was cutting off her circulation. "She doesn't look too happy."

"We didn't want to tell you until after the wedding, but your sister won't be here today. She left a note. Lisa has eloped with some man we've never heard of."

Francie glanced around, noting for the first time that her sister was a no show and thought "Damn!" She did her best to look suitably surprised by the news.

Lisa had done it. She'd eloped. And the shit was going to hit the fan, but it wouldn't be blowing in her direction for a change.

"Lisa's a grown woman. I'm sure she knows what she's doing." That thought was ludicrous at best, not to mention downright hysterical.

"Your sister has made your mother and I very upset, but we are not going to let her selfishness ruin your day, Francie."

The music began, signaling to Francie and her father that it was show time.

John leaned down and kissed his daughter's cheek. "I'm very proud of you this day, *cara*. Mark is a great guy. You made the right decision to marry him."

"Thanks, Pop! It wasn't that difficult of a decision to make. I'm in love."

If her smile grew any wider, she'd been tagged as mentally deranged, Francie thought. *Thank you, Dr. Rosenblat!*

She headed down the aisle to where Mark was waiting for her with a huge smile on his face and love in his eyes.

I love you, he mouthed, then winked at her.

Her heart did a complete flip-flop, and she heaved a sigh of happiness. "Ain't love grand?"

And it was.